Dead Wrong

Dead Wrong

An Amish Cozy Mystery

By
Vannetta Chapman

Agatha's Amish B&B Series, Book 1

DEAD WRONG

Cover design: Seedlingsonline
Interior design: Henscratches.com

First printing, 2019

ASIN: B07X7HNDDG

Dedicated to
Russell Dixon

"Give, and it will be given to you.
A good measure,
pressed down, shaken together and running over,
will be poured into your lap.
For with the measure you use, it will be measured
to you."
Luke 6:38 (NIV)

"There is nothing on this earth more to be prized
than true friendship."
Thomas Aquinas

Glossary

Abuela—grandmother
Boppli-baby
Bruder—brother
Dat—dad
Danki—thank you
Englischer—non-Amish person
Fraa—wife
Freinden—friends
Gotte—God
Grandkinner—grandchildren
Grossdaddi—grandfather
Gude mariye—good morning
Gut—good
Kapp—prayer covering
Kind—child
Mamm—mom
Narrisch—crazy
Nein—no
Onkel—uncle
Ordnung—unwritten rules of the community
(literally "orders")
Schweschder—sister
Ya—yes
Youngie—young adult or teenager

Prologue

August, 20__
Hunt, Texas

AGATHA LAPP CHANGED buses three times travelling from Shipshewana, Indiana to central Texas. Once she arrived in San Antonio, she hired a taxi, and finally was picked up by the bishop in the small community of Hunt.

"Long trip." Jonas Schrock was younger than most bishops she'd known, though his beard was peppered with gray.

She guessed they were close to the same age — she'd turned fifty-five six weeks earlier.

It felt relaxing to be in a buggy again. Jonas's horse seemed to appreciate the cloudless summer day, and the sound of its hooves against the pavement soothed her frazzled nerves.

"I'm definitely not in Indiana anymore." She'd come down to Texas the previous spring. Of course, she had. Her youngest *bruder* had died, tragically, along with his wife of just two years. They hadn't had children yet. She supposed there was mercy in that, although she would have happily taken on the responsibility of raising a niece or nephew, same as she was now taking on the business Samuel had left behind.

"Texas takes a bit of getting used to." Jonas glanced out over the buggy horse, waved to the right and left. "But it's *gut* land, and with the river..."

"What's the name of it...something with a G?"

"Guadalupe. The river's so close to town, it runs directly behind many of our properties, including Samuel's. It was a *gut* place for us to settle."

Agatha tried to see the beauty Jonas was describing, but the temperature had to be over a hundred and there was no breeze to speak of.

"It's hot," she finally admitted.

"*Ya*. That it is. Must have been pleasant when you left Indiana."

"Seventy-five." She didn't sigh. Agatha couldn't abide people who sighed dramatically. The weather was what it was. What *Gotte* had created it to be. She would learn to live with the Texas heat.

"I wanted to thank you, again, for seeing after

their place until I could move. I had...some things to take care of." It was unusual for an Amish woman, even a widowed one, to move away on her own. She didn't intend to go into that now, though. If Jonas was worried, he'd speak with her bishop back in Shipshe, and Atlee had understood her decision and given his blessing.

"It was no bother, and I'm sure you'd do the same. My son took your buggy horse over to your place earlier today."

"A mare?"

"*Ya*. Her name is Doc."

"My *bruder* named a mare Doc?"

Jonas's laugh was rich and deep. "Samuel loved Dr. Pepper."

"I've never heard of it."

"It's a type of soft drink—originated here in Texas. Samuel drank it fairly often. When he and Deborah moved here, he made her a deal. She could name the children, and he'd name the horses and dogs."

A lump formed in her throat. She had to swallow around it to say, "He never told me that."

"He named the horse Dr. Pepper, which Deborah argued was much too long."

"And they shortened it to Doc."

"We made sure the barn is cleaned out and you have supplies."

"*Danki*."

"The property though…it's going to need some cleaning up. I'd be happy to schedule a work day."

Agatha waved away that idea. She didn't mind hard work. Wasn't that why she'd come down here? Knitting and quilting were good and fine, but she needed a purpose. She needed something that would wear her out and make her sleep well at night. She needed…well, she supposed she needed to be needed, even if it was only to strangers looking for a place to stay. Running Samuel's bed and breakfast would provide all those things.

"The community is doing well?"

"*Ya*. Seems like we add a new family every month, and the *Englischers*—they realize we're bringing in more tourist dollars so they're accommodating."

Agatha pulled a handkerchief from her purse and swiped at the sweat running down her face. "How long does this heat last?"

"Three, maybe four months." He laughed when he said it. "Some years a little longer. We were fortunate in that we had a fairly cool May, but fall comes late here and doesn't stick around long."

"Surely we don't get snow this far south."

"*Nein*. Not usually, but the temperatures can drop to freezing in the winter and it can be damp."

Anything below triple digits sounded heavenly to her.

They'd passed through the center of town

and popped out the other side. The surrounding hills rose gently on all sides, and the trees were magnificent. She could see why people would want to vacation here.

"Your place is just ahead on the left."

She craned her neck. Though she'd seen it before, had even stayed there during the funeral, she wondered if she'd perhaps imagined how pretty it was. But now, here was the lane and the long, low ranch house with a porch on three sides. It stretched invitingly across the front of the house which faced west, wrapped around to the north so that it faced her neighbor there, and then continued across the back. Yes, it was as pretty as she remembered, though as Jonas had warned it was in need of some tender, loving care.

The grass was knee high, and the place looked deserted—which it was. The sign which read **AMISH B&B** was hanging by one chain. She'd need to fix that straight away.

Jonas pulled the buggy to a stop near the steps that led the way to the front porch. As he removed her luggage—two small bags because all she'd brought was her clothing—she stepped closer to the house and ran a hand along the peeling paint of the porch railing.

"Place needs work." Jonas used the toe of his shoe to right a pot holding a dead plant. "Samuel and Deborah were *gut* people, hard workers, too, but they seemed somewhat at a loss regarding how to run a business."

Agatha walked to the corner of the house, then stepped away from it a bit so she could see the yard gently sloping down to the river. It was peaceful and quite gorgeous—like something out of a dream. "Samuel was the youngest in our family. We spoiled him a bit. He was more likely to have his line in the water than he was to finish plowing a field."

"He loved to fish," Jonas agreed.

"As for Deborah...well, she was ten years younger and inexperienced in the workings of the world. Or she seemed that way to me."

Jonas nodded, adding, "Their life was complete."

"Indeed."

It was the Amish way to accept death and even to celebrate it in light of eternity. And yet, it was hard when the person who died was a member of your own family. She shook away her morose thoughts. The best way to honor Samuel's life, and Deborah's, was by making their business successful.

"Would you like me to go inside with you? The ladies put clean linens on the bed and brought over a little food. There's fresh milk and eggs, some bread, and basic staples."

"I appreciate the offer very much, but I suspect that you have things to do at home. I know the life of a bishop is a busy one."

He didn't argue. Instead, he reached out a hand and placed it ever-so-gently on the top of her *kapp*. "Heavenly Father, bless this child of Yours as she goes about her work—give her strength of body, mind, and spirit. Guide and direct her, and fill her with the peace that You so freely share."

For reasons Agatha didn't want to examine, the blessing brought tears to her eyes. As the bishop drove away, her mind filled with the dozens of things she needed to do—check on the mare, put away her clothes, fix herself something to eat, mow the grass. But she didn't do any of those things. Instead, she walked around the porch, still covered in leaves from last fall. A dilapidated swing looked as if it would collapse if she sat on it. Two rockers near the front window didn't look much better.

She continued around the side of the house and sat down on the steps, looking east toward the river. Her neighbor drove his pickup truck down the lane that separated their property and into his carport. Situated on the south side of the house, the covered parking area consisted of enough space for two vehicles and a back wall that looked as if it held a closet of sorts. The entire structure was attached to the house by a short, covered walk. As he exited his pickup, Agatha saw that he was Hispanic and looked to be sixty. He glanced her way but didn't seem surprised to see her there.

Or maybe he didn't see her.

He didn't raise a hand or call out. Instead, he pulled a single bag of groceries from the back seat and trudged into his house. *Trudge* was the only word for it. He looked as if he was carrying a dreadful weight on his shoulders.

A yellow cat poked its head out from under the porch and hissed at her.

"If you want scraps from me, you're going to have to behave better than that."

Instead of answering, the cat walked to a patch of sunlight, sat, and commenced cleaning itself.

Agatha sometimes had trouble believing she was fifty-five years old. She'd lost her husband ten years ago, and her children had long since married and moved away. It seemed as if the last thirty years of her life had passed in a blink. Now she was starting over in a new community doing something she'd never done before. She understood hard work, and she was fully aware that making a success from Samuel's dream wasn't going to be easy. In truth, she knew nothing about running a Bed-and-Breakfast.

But she knew about cleaning and feeding people and needing a place to slow down and reconnect with God. She knew all about those things.

A fish slapped the water.

Sunlight pierced the pecan trees.

A gentle breeze cooled the sweat on her brow.

"This could be a *gut* place."

The cat didn't argue.

Chapter One

Ten months later

*A*GATHA PAUSED a moment on the steps of her back porch. She carried fresh bed linens and towels for Cabin 3 which she shifted to her left arm, touched her *kapp* to be sure it was in place, and tugged on her apron. She should be in a hurry, as the sun was slanting toward the horizon and tonight her B&B was again filled to capacity.

But she wasn't in a hurry.

A chicken casserole warmed in the oven, and fresh baked bread sat cooling on the kitchen counter.

The June day would be a long one, so she'd pushed dinner to 6:30.

And what was the point of living in the

off the porch and started down the path, which was when she spied the Beilers and Glicks, checking out the tennis courts—soon to be shuffleboard courts. And there were the Fishers, sitting in the gazebo and laughing about something. Ella and James had about the sunniest dispositions Agatha had ever encountered. Those two might be in their eighties, but they certainly embraced life.

Agatha hurried down the path carrying the towering pile of fresh linens. Fonzi lay in the sun, curled like the letter U. She'd inherited the yellow cat with the property.

Cabin 1, where the Fishers were staying, was in good shape. Ella Fisher had even made the bed and hung up the towels, indicating that she didn't expect clean linens. Agatha wrote *Thank You* and a smiley face on the white board near the door.

Cabin 2 was a different story. The Cox brothers were staying there, no doubt because they could spread out. There were two full sized beds, a small kitchen with a table for four, and a nice-sized sitting area. It was one of Agatha's favorite cabins because she could imagine it being a little house for someone. Only, at the moment, it was housing more fishing gear than the local sports store.

Fishing vests, waders, tackle boxes, and poles covered every available surface. The kitchen table was staging what looked like a fly-tying competition. As for the cooking area, it didn't appear to have been touched. Mason and Paxton were getting by on granola bars and the two meals a day she provided. She walked over to the refrigerator, opened the freezer, and was a bit surprised to see no fish there — none in the refrigerator portion either.

They obviously hadn't cooked any, as the dishes hadn't been used and the stove was still immaculate. Those boys had been fishing for the better part of two days. Had they caught nothing? She'd have to ask them. If they weren't having any luck, she'd ask Charlie Knox to stop by. Charlie knew all the fishing tips for their area, and he didn't mind dispensing a few of them in exchange for one of Agatha's fresh pies.

Her business depended on repeat customers. The last thing she wanted was for two avid fishermen to go home empty-handed.

She quickly changed the bed linens, dropping the dirty sheets and towels onto the front porch of the cabin to pick up on her way back to the main house.

One more cabin to service and she could turn her attentions to putting the finishing touches on dinner.

Cabin 3 sat a little farther down the path and around the bend. Perhaps that's why Mr. Dixon had chosen it. He seemed to value his privacy. Agatha stepped onto the porch but paused outside the front door. She clearly stated that the rooms would be serviced in the afternoon between three and five, but there was always the possibility that Mr. Dixon had decided to take a late afternoon nap.

Nothing worse than walking in on a guest who was fast asleep, snoring with his mouth wide open and his glasses askew. She'd learned that lesson the first week she'd reopened the B&B.

Knocking firmly on the door, she called out, "Anyone home? Agatha Lapp here."

No answer.

Well, she hadn't thought there would be.

It was a beautiful June afternoon. Why would anyone be inside?

She tried the door on the off chance it had been left unlocked.

Definitely locked, and the curtains were drawn tight as well. Agatha called out one more time, then reached into the pocket of her apron and fetched her master key. Slipping it into the lock, she pushed the door open with what she hoped was a friendly, "Anyone home? Just here to change the..."

She never did finish that sentence.

Her mind reeled, trying to make sense of the scene before her.

Mr. Dixon's suitcase had been flung open and clothes tossed around the room. The breakfast tray she'd left on the porch earlier that morning sat on the nightstand by the bed, though the mug had been knocked over and lay shattered on the floor. The bedding had been dragged toward the open back door. She glanced around as if Mr. Dixon might pop out from the broom closet.

But there was no sign of the man.

No indication of what had happened.

She stepped toward the back door and peered outside, which was when her knees began to shake. She reached for the doorframe with one hand as her other fluttered to her chest and pressed against it to slow the hammering of her heart.

She simply couldn't make the details of what she was seeing fit together into a cohesive picture— Russell Dixon lying face down at the edge of the clearing, one hand trapped beneath him and the other reaching over his head. The unnatural position confirmed what her mind couldn't accept.

Mr. Dixon wouldn't be caring if she changed his linens because Mr. Dixon was literally dead to the world.

✽

sure…I can't believe it, but he's dead." Why was she out of breath? She hadn't climbed a mountain. She'd run fifty yards, maybe less.

"Sit down. Let me get you a glass of water."

"*Nein.* He's…he's dead, and I…I don't know what I'm supposed to do."

Vargas was in his sixties, recently retired from what she'd heard, and suddenly alone after the death of his wife. His skin was brown like a well-seasoned saddle. He rarely smiled, but his eyes seemed kind though sad. At Agatha's proclamation, he nodded as if what she said made sense, though she realized it probably didn't. He ducked back inside, grabbed his phone, and then dashed toward Cabin 3.

Agatha sat there, leaning forward so that her head hung between her knees. She'd never fainted, but she'd read the occasional romance novel which assured readers this was the way to slow the rush of blood to your head.

When her pulse finally calmed, she sat up and looked around. She'd never been on her neighbor's back porch; she'd taken him a peach pie once but that had been delivered to his front door. He'd accepted it quietly, thanked her, and firmly shut the door on her.

Mr. Vargas wasn't the neighborly type.

So why had she run to him for help?

Who else was she supposed to run to? It wasn't like she knew what to do with a dead body.

Had Russell Dixon actually been dead?

How was that possible?

She couldn't answer any of those questions, so instead, she prayed. She prayed for Mr. Vargas, that he would know what to do and that no harm would come to him. She prayed for her guests, that they wouldn't be alarmed by this strange turn of events. She prayed for herself that she'd have wisdom for whatever lay ahead; and finally, she prayed for the soul of Russell Dixon.

She opened her eyes to see Mr. Vargas sprinting back across the yard. She jumped up and waited at the porch railing. "Is he…"

One quick nod vanquished any hopes she'd been clinging to that she had been mistaken.

"Mr. Vargas…"

"Antonio. My name is Antonio. Most folks just call me Tony."

"And I'm Agatha. I met you before when I first moved in. I don't know if you remember."

"You're still shaking. It's the adrenaline. Sit down, and I'll get you a glass of water. Or maybe you'd like something stronger?"

"*Nein*. I'm…I'm Amish."

He nodded, strode into the house, and returned with a glass of water, which he pushed into her hands.

"*Danki*, but I need to get back to my guests."

"I asked everyone to move into the house and

told them to wait there. I told them we'd explain everything soon."

"And Mr. Dixon?"

"Dead. I called 9-1-1. The authorities will be here any minute."

"I appreciate your help. I don't normally lose my head like that."

"Your first dead body?"

"What? Yes, of course."

"Then it's understandable." He cupped his hand beneath her elbow and guided her back to a chair, then nodded toward the glass of water in her hands. "Drink. It'll help."

She didn't think she'd be able to stomach anything, not even the cup of water, but she drank the entire thing down in one long pull.

"Better?"

"Maybe...yes." Agatha swiped at a strand of hair that had fallen out of her *kapp*. Was it only a few minutes ago that she'd stood on her back porch delighting in the beauty of the afternoon?

One minute passed, then two. Tony didn't rush her, and she gradually grew calmer.

"I don't know why I ran here. I'm sorry..."

Antonio waved away her apology. "When adrenaline surges through your system, your body goes into fight-or-flight mode."

"I'm Amish..."

"Yes, you mentioned that."

"So I have no experience with fighting."

"Hence the flight."

They waited in silence another few minutes and then the sound of sirens split the quiet of the afternoon. They both turned to stare at the cruisers barreling down the road with lights flashing.

"Would you like me to go with you?"

"Please."

Which was how she found herself walking toward the front of her home and a group of *Englisch* police officers with Tony Vargas at her side.

Chapter Three

Tony shook hands with Lieutenant Bannister.
"Detective."

"Lieutenant."

Agatha stared at him, then at the emergency personnel assembling on her lawn—two police cruisers, three officers plus the lieutenant, and an ambulance with two EMS workers. She still seemed to be in shock judging by the way she kept clutching her right arm to her side to stop its trembling. And her pupils remained dilated, a sure sign adrenaline continued to pump through her system.

Tony cleared his throat and took charge, something he hadn't done in over four years. "The deceased is at the back of the property. Follow the path to the last cabin, and you'll find him ten yards from the back door."

Bannister's hand went to the butt of his gun.

"No sign of foul play."

"Heart attack?"

Tony shrugged. He didn't like making any assumptions this early in a case, not that a dead guest on his neighbor's property made it his case.

"Witnesses?"

"I moved all the other guests inside and asked them to wait for further instructions. This is Agatha Lapp, the owner of the Bed-and-Breakfast."

"We'll need to interview you in a few minutes."

Agatha nodded, though she didn't offer to shake Bannister's hand—whether that was because she was Amish or some other reason, Tony didn't know.

The EMS personnel were already moving toward the back of the house.

Bannister addressed two of his officers. "Check the perimeter of the property, just to be sure."

He motioned for the person riding shotgun with him to step closer. The officer was probably in her thirties, physically fit, and Antonio was pretty sure that if he checked, he'd find she was still wet behind the ears. But she was wearing the department uniform, and she was a member of the lieutenant's staff, so she must have earned the position.

Bannister wasn't yet fifty. He was close to six feet and looked as if he could drop and rip off a hundred push-ups. He'd spent some years in the military and retained habits learned there. His pants had a sharp crease down the middle, his hair was buzz cut, and he didn't mince words. "Call dispatch. Ask them to send out..."

He turned to Agatha. "How many guests do you have on the property today?"

"Other than Mr. Dixon, there are twelve adults, a baby, and myself."

"And Mr. Dixon is the deceased?"

Agatha nodded her head once, a quick jerky movement.

"Tami, get me thirteen witness forms. Have Jolene bring them out stat." Again addressing Agatha, he said, "You can go inside, Mrs. Lapp. We'll be in soon, but for now please keep your guests inside the building. I don't need people traipsing over a potential crime scene."

Agatha glanced at Tony, no doubt wondering at the lieutenant's use of the phrase *crime scene*. A rookie mistake, though Bannister had plenty of experience. He'd been on the force nearly ten years. He'd made detective when Tony left and risen to lieutenant shortly after that.

But calling the area a crime scene? That was unnecessary. There was no need to further frighten the person who'd found the deceased.

"I can go inside with you," Tony offered.

Agatha pressed a hand to her throat. "*Danki*.

I'd appreciate that."

They traipsed across her front yard and up the steps.

Tony hadn't been in the sprawling ranch home since it had been converted to a B&B. He was surprised at how much better it looked than when the Beans had owned it. Flowers overflowed brightly colored pots strategically positioned on the porch steps. Healthy ferns hung from the porch ceiling. The old porch swing had been replaced, and freshly-painted rocking chairs sported bright colored pillows.

The Bed-and-Breakfast didn't look like your typical murder scene, but after thirty years on the police force, Tony knew there was no such thing. Every murder was different and every scene held unique challenges—secrets even, though he wasn't ready to jump to the conclusion that there had been a murder. Russell Dixon might have died from natural causes. There were a few things about the cabin that bothered him—the cabin and the man's final resting position.

They stepped into the house and Tony was nearly knocked over by the aroma of fresh baked bread, some sort of casserole, and if he wasn't mistaken, apple pie. A new case had always spurred his appetite.

Not your case, he silently reminded himself.

Agatha led him into the adjacent room—a

living room situated at the front of the house—and twelve guests turned to stare at them. The questions came all at once, tumbling over each other and demanding answers.

"What's happened?"

"Why are the police here?"

"Did I hear someone say 'crime scene?'"

"What crime? Are we in danger?"

Tony opened his mouth to address their concerns, but it seemed the moment Agatha stepped into her Bed-and-Breakfast she took on the role of mother hen. The frightened, disheveled woman who'd appeared on his back porch vanished—at least for the moment.

Her conservative dress had first caused him to think she was older, but on closer look she appeared younger than he was and physically fit. Running a Bed-and-Breakfast no doubt helped in that area. Agatha Lapp looked to be in her early fifties and stood about five and a half feet. Brown hair just beginning to turn gray peeking out from the white bonnet she wore.

Agatha moved to the center of the room. "Have a seat, everyone."

Complete silence settled over the group— stunned silence, as if they were waiting to hear the other shoe drop.

"I'm happy to tell you what I know, but first… can I get anyone a soda or cup of tea? I'm afraid dinner is going to be delayed. I have some freshly baked cookies..."

By asking such normal, run-of-the-mill questions, Agatha inadvertently calmed the situation. The three Amish couples sat down. The young woman holding a baby moved to a rocking chair, her husband opting to stand behind her. The black couple moved closer to one another. Only the two men, still wearing their waders and dripping water all over Agatha's wood floor, remained at the window.

When Agatha asked one of the Amish women to help her in the kitchen, everyone resumed speaking in low voices. Tony walked over to the two fishermen. "Perhaps you could step out on the porch and remove the waders."

"What?" The taller of the two looked around as if he didn't understand what Tony was referring to.

"We're dripping, bro. All over Agatha's floor." The shorter brother—and they had to be brothers because they were carbon copies except for the difference in height—stuck out his hand for Tony to shake. "Name's Paxton. Paxton Cox. And this is my clueless older brother Mason."

Mason's gaze had been darting around, and when he glanced back toward them, Tony noted that his pupils were dilated and his breathing seemed a bit ragged. He acted almost as if he'd been the one to find Dixon.

Tony shook hands with Mason and couldn't help but notice that his palms were sweaty. What was that about? "You were fly fishing?"

"We were." Paxton's head bobbed up and down. "We have been since we got here yesterday. So it's okay for us to step out on the porch?"

"Sure. Just stick close."

"Of course. Wouldn't want to get arrested."

Which seemed a strange thing to say, but what was even stranger was the way Mason glared at his younger brother, then strode out onto the porch without another word. Paxton shrugged and followed him.

Tony popped into the kitchen where Agatha and two of her guests were arranging mugs on one serving platter and cookies on another. "Do you have a towel? Your fishing guests dripped water all over the floor."

Agatha fetched an old threadbare one from the cabinet under the kitchen sink. "Will this work?"

"Perfectly."

He couldn't get over how she'd calmed since entering the house. Obviously, it was her sanctuary—a place she felt at home and comfortable. He could understand why. The last of the afternoon light streamed through the large windows. A kitchen nook on the east side of the room held window seats that looked out toward the river. The freshly-painted white cabinets and uncluttered counters sparkled.

By the time he'd wiped the water from the floor, the Cox brothers were back in the room and Agatha had served drinks and snacks to everyone who wanted something.

The young couple with the baby introduced themselves as Stuart and Brooklyn Willis. Brooklyn was average height, thin, with blonde hair pulled back in a ponytail. She looked tired, but then he supposed most new mothers did. Stuart seemed the geeky type—large glasses, pale skin, and wearing a t-shirt that read *Keep Calm and Reboot*. Baby Hudson was six months old and sucking on a pacifier that took up the entire lower portion of his face.

Stuart, who remained standing behind his wife's chair, was the first to speak. "This is nice and all, and we appreciate your hospitality, Agatha. But what's going on? Are we in danger?"

"No one's in danger, Stuart." Agatha sat perched on the edge of a straight back chair. "One of the guests—Mr. Dixon—has died."

Which started everyone talking at once again.

Agatha raised a hand to shush them, and Tony was surprised when they complied. But then she stared down at her hands, apparently at a loss for words. Finally, she glanced over at Tony, and he stepped forward. "Let Agatha explain, and then if you have any questions that I can answer, I'd be happy to do so."

An older Amish gentleman ran his fingers

Paxton asked. "No offense, Agatha. But we came here to fish, not sit around and eat cookies."

Agatha looked to Tony for the answer, so he moved in front of the fireplace and addressed the group. "What the officers are doing now is standard procedure for a 10-39."

"Ten what?" Xavier asked.

"Report of a dead person. Each police department has its own protocol in such a situation — steps they follow, which includes obtaining a witness statement from each of you. Since this appears to be a fairly open and shut case..." A twinge of guilt caused him to pause. He did have questions about what he'd seen, but they were probably easily explained. *And this isn't my case.* "It shouldn't take more than an hour or two, and then you all can go on about your vacation."

That seemed to settle everyone down. Ten minutes later Jolene arrived with the witness forms, and Tami directed each couple into separate rooms to fill them out.

"Another standard operating procedure?" Agatha asked.

"Pretty much."

"So they can't...corrupt each other's testimony?"

"This isn't a murder investigation, Agatha. I don't know what you've seen on television, but this isn't that."

"I'm Amish, Tony."

"So you mentioned."

"I don't watch television. We don't use electricity."

"None at all?"

"I did have it installed in the cabins for the guests."

"Oh." Glancing around, he realized that must be one of the reasons the place looked so clean—no televisions, computers, stereo systems. In fact, it reminded him of his *abuela*'s home.

"So why do they need to be separated?"

"Because we're all very open to suggestion. That conversation we had earlier? Where you told everyone how you found Dixon? It probably shouldn't have happened, but I didn't feel like it was my place to stop you."

"I rather wish you had."

"People think the memory works like a video recorder." He stopped, glanced around again, then asked, "Uh…do you know about video recorders?"

"I don't own one, but I know how they work."

"Okay, well, obviously a device can record events and then play them back exactly as they occurred."

"But the human mind doesn't work that way."

"Not at all. Our memories are reconstructed." He spied a table tucked into the corner of the room with a half assembled jigsaw puzzle of a cat in a garden. "Like that puzzle. We put the pieces together, and the way we do so is susceptible to the way other people do so."

"Like you put a puzzle together based on the picture on the box."

"Exactly. Only in the case of Mr. Dixon's death, we don't know what the picture on the box looks like yet. That's what the detective has to do—put together an accurate picture of what happened."

"And you're a detective?"

"I was, but I'm not anymore."

Chapter Four

THREE HOURS later Agatha watched the paramedics roll Russell Dixon's body to the waiting ambulance. He was covered with a sheet, of course. The emergency personnel loaded him up, then jumped into the ambulance and drove away—at a much more sedate speed than they'd arrived and without the siren blaring. Russell Dixon wasn't in a hurry. It wouldn't matter how long they took to deliver him to the county morgue.

Had it really only been a few hours since she'd found him? How life could turn on a dime.

She stood watching, her Bible in one hand and a basket of food in the other. Tony walked over and said something to the lieutenant. Those two seemed like oil and water. Lieutenant Bannister reminded her of a peacock her neighbors in Shipshe had once owned. The thing would strut around with its feathers spread wide and cry like a baby. She'd been rather relieved when they donated it to a local zoo.

Antonio Vargas, on the other hand, looked like a man who had just strolled onto her property. Warm brown skin, black hair sprinkled with gray, and brown eyes that caused her to wonder what had happened to him. Tony looked for all the world like a man who'd woken abruptly from a long nap and found himself dropped into the river of life.

She thought back to the day she'd moved to Hunt. The property had been in a state of disrepair and she'd been exhausted by the long trip to Texas. Not ready to face what was on the inside of the house, she walked around the porch and sat on the steps to watch the river flowing by her property. Tony drove down the drive that separated their two homes, parked in his carport, and trudged into the house. He'd looked exhausted even then.

He still looked exhausted.

As if he sensed the direction of her thoughts, he turned now and walked toward the front porch. She met him at the steps, a book in one hand and a basket in the other. She handed him the basket.

"For me?" His eyebrows shot up as he peeked under the dishtowel.

"You worked with the officers while we ate."

"You didn't have to do this."

"I think you rather earned it."

Tony tucked the cloth back around the dinner. "Would you like to sit for a minute?"

She led him over to the rockers. A rocking chair could soothe her soul when few other things could. The cat immediately jumped down from the window sill and began winding his way through her legs.

"You've already been fed, Fonzi."

"Fonzi?"

"Gina—my friend—named him. He came with the house, and we've become *gut freinden*." As if to prove her point, the cat dropped on the porch floor and rolled onto his back, paws in the air, a soft purr emanating from him.

Agatha rubbed his belly, then glanced up at Tony. "Who was the man in the blue sedan?"

"Our county ME—Medical Examiner."

"And why was he called?"

"In Texas, if there's an unattended death, then it's standard procedure to bring in the ME. His name is Scott Millican. He's a good guy."

Agatha blinked rapidly. She patted both of her pockets then the top of her head to locate her glasses. She only needed them to read. She was always leaving them laying about, which was one of the problems with only needing them for certain tasks. She'd like to open the Bible in her hand and

Tony nodded. "He was barefoot when you found him, so that's possible."

"But why would he go out the back door, and why wouldn't he put on his shoes?"

Tony shrugged, which she was learning was his way of saying, *go on*.

"Okay. Well, the covers were thrown back. It definitely looked like he'd slept there. His clothing was...tossed everywhere. I didn't spend much time looking at the room because the back door was open, and I thought that was odd."

"Wide open or ajar?"

"Wide open, as if someone had thrown it open."

He motioned with his hand for her to continue.

"I saw him...saw him almost as soon as I looked outside. We only mow about ten feet out from the cabin. The natural grasses, they bring in birds like roadrunners and bobwhite quail. Anyway, beyond the perimeter of the cabin, the grass is quite tall, nearly waist high. He was lying in it, and I couldn't see most of him. But his foot was sticking out onto the mowed part, as if—well, as if he'd been standing there and someone had pushed him over."

"Anything else?"

"*Nein*. Except..." She rubbed her eyes, suddenly realizing how desperately tired she felt. But she wanted to get this right, wanted to see *her* memory—not one she might have reconstructed from hearing the others talking. She took a deep breath, pushed aside thoughts of a hot cup of tea and questions over whether this would be bad for business and what would that poor man's family think when they learned he'd passed. She began at the bottom of the steps and walked back through the cabin.

"The breakfast tray."

"What about it?"

"I left it on the porch steps early that morning. Dixon had fetched it and placed it on the nightstand beside the bed, but the mug...the mug was shattered on the floor." Her eyes popped open. "And the bedding...it wasn't thrown back. Someone—I suppose Mr. Dixon—had dragged it toward the open back door. Why would he do that?"

"Something startled him perhaps."

"Or someone." Agatha's mouth went suddenly dry. "If you jumped up out of bed, wouldn't you throw the covers back? And why was the mug broken?"

Tony ran a hand up and down his jaw line. Finally, he said, "I didn't mean to upset you."

She rubbed the palm of her hand over the smooth oak of the rocking chair's arm and admitted, "It's been a long day."

"I won't keep you then." Tony stood, picked up the basket, and walked toward the steps. He turned back toward her before she'd even risen from the rocking chair. "If you see or hear anything…"

"Like what?"

"Anything at all, Agatha."

It occurred to her that it was the first time he'd used her name, and why did he suddenly look so concerned?

"If you see or hear anything, come and get me."

Without any other explanation, he stepped out into the darkening night.

Chapter Five

AGATHA WOKE the next morning just before the crack of dawn, as was her custom. But this time she opened her eyes with a sense of foreboding, and at first, she couldn't figure out why. The memories of finding Russell Dixon returned like waves crashing on a beach.

If there was one thing she'd learned through her own troubles it was that dwelling on tragedy was never beneficial. So she went through her normal routine of dressing quickly and tidying her personal quarters, which consisted of a bedroom, bath, and living area. The small office she left for Gina to clean. Within twenty minutes she was drinking her first cup of coffee on the side porch where she could watch the river.

Fonzi sat cleaning his face after having consumed his breakfast rather quickly. No doubt he'd prowled about most of the night.

The view of the river didn't give her the peace it usually did. She had trouble focusing on the beauty before her. Her gaze repeatedly turned toward Tony's house.

She'd lived in Hunt almost a year, and she didn't really know the man at all.

Yet she'd run to him when she was frightened.

Why had she done that?

A light was on in his kitchen, so either Tony was up or he'd left it on all night. She found herself praying for her neighbor, and for Russell Dixon's family, and even for her guests, that they would not be unnecessarily traumatized by the previous day's events.

It wasn't her job to solve the mystery of Dixon's death—if it was a mystery. So instead, she went inside, poured herself another cup of coffee, and sat down at the kitchen table with a pad of paper and pencil. She always began each day with a to-do list. It freed up her mind to focus on other things.

She'd need to get in contact with Gina and ask if she could come out and take care of Cabin 3. Gina Phillips did basic house cleaning for her and helped with the shopping since she was *Englisch* and owned a car. But more than that, she'd become a good friend, and Agatha found her mood improving at the thought of seeing her. Gina pretended to be grumpy, but she always expressed it in such a funny way that they both ended up laughing. Gina would have a better perspective on all that had happened.

Agatha had pre-made all the dinners for the week, so she'd only have to pop tonight's casserole into the oven. If things went well, she'd have time to work in the small vegetable garden she kept next to the barn and catch up on the knitting project she'd planned to work on the day before—her niece was expecting another grandbaby before summer's end. The family had seven girls and desperately hoped for a boy, though in their letters they claimed an eighth girl would be just fine too.

She was finishing her list and was about to pop the morning's pecan cinnamon rolls into the oven when Jasmine and Xavier walked into the room. The couple lived in the Houston area and had only been married a few months.

"I'm surprised to see you two up so early. This is your vacation. Aren't you supposed to be sleeping in?"

"That was the idea." Xavier blinked his eyes several times, as if he wasn't quite sure how he'd ended up in the kitchen.

Jasmine, on the other hand, looked wide awake. "We wanted to come down and talk to you, while you were still alone."

Agatha felt her eyebrows shoot up. "Let me

just fix you some coffee first."

She took her time filling the mugs and gathering up sugar and cream. Jasmine looked as if she needed a few minutes to center her thoughts, and Xavier looked as if he wished he were still upstairs in bed.

When everyone was clutching hot mugs, Jasmine said, "It's about Mr. Dixon. I remembered something, and well...I didn't know if we should go back to that Lieutenant Bannister and tell him. I don't mind saying he seemed a little full of himself. I've met plenty of officers like him in my life, and I'm not saying that because I'm black."

"Jasmine..."

She held up a hand to stop her husband's protests. "I won't sugarcoat it, and you shouldn't either. There are plenty of good officers—both black and white, but I've met my share of officers who take their position a little too seriously. Bannister seemed like just that sort of man."

She stared down into her mug for a moment, finally took a long sip and closed her eyes as if the caffeine was ministering to her heart and mind as well as her body. When she glanced at Agatha again, she admitted, "I was hoping we could just speak with you."

"Hmmm." Agatha turned her mug left and then right as she glanced toward the window. Tony's truck drove past. Where was he going at six in the morning? Not that it was any of her business.

She turned her attention back to her guests. "Why don't you tell me what you remembered, and then we can decide together whether we should inform Lieutenant Bannister."

Jasmine jerked her head up and down, reminding Agatha of one of those bobble-head dolls, took another gulp of the coffee, and pushed the mug away. "We saw him yesterday morning. It was early. Remember we went on that hike to Lost Maples yesterday so we were up before sunrise."

"Two days in a row," Xavier muttered.

"I happened to glance out the window, and I saw Mr. Dixon. There was enough light to make out who it was, though the sun wasn't fully up yet. Anyway...he was leaving Cabin 2."

The muscles along the back of Agatha's neck tightened immediately. She rolled her shoulders before saying, "You must be mistaken. Mr. Dixon was staying in Cabin 3."

"I know, and I can't see Cabin 3 from my window. It's around the bend. But the yard slopes down, and I have a perfect view of Cabin 2—I have an unobstructed view of the front porch to Cabin 2."

"And this was early yesterday morning?"

"A few minutes after six." Jasmine glanced out the window and visibly shivered. "About this time."

Xavier sat back, putting his arm across the back of Jasmine's chair. "My wife has an overactive imagination. She's intent on turning this into a

"I'll run this by Tony. He seemed to be familiar with the process…"

"Yeah, it's handy that you have a retired detective living next door." Xavier frowned as he leaned back in his chair.

"Trust me, that is not something I plan on needing in the future. But yes, in this instance it is handy. Now let me fetch breakfast. You two look like you could use some comfort food."

❋

Chapter Six

Tony hadn't stepped through the doors of the Hunt Police Department since his retirement four years earlier. He knew some people missed their work and had trouble adjusting to life without a purpose. He'd had plenty of purpose in his life until Camilla had died.

He'd been stuck in neutral since then, and he didn't mind admitting it. Nothing appealed to him—not fishing in the river or visiting his *abuela* or taking out the $40,000 Airstream he and Camilla had bought to see the country. He sold the RV six months after she died and didn't miss it one bit. What did he care about seeing the Cascade Mountains if Camilla wasn't by his side? Or the Grand Canyon or Niagara Falls or any of the places on their list?

Nothing had interested him—until now.

The situation at Agatha's had woken him before it was properly light. Habits die hard. He supposed thirty years of working in law enforcement didn't stop just because a person retired. There were things about Russell Dixon's death that didn't sit right. So instead of stewing over the questions building in his mind, he decided to have a chat with Lieutenant Bannister.

The man was already sitting behind his desk, as Tony had known he would be. There had never been a question that Jimmy Bannister was committed to the job.

"Tony. I'm surprised to see you this early." He motioned to the chair across from his desk, across from what had been Tony's desk.

Tony looked around. Four years and little had changed. Boxes of files still stacked on the floor— probably the same boxes of files. The blinds over the windows still needed dusting. For all he knew, it was the same coffee cup sitting on the desk. The only real difference was the framed photos on the wall. Bannister shaking hands with the mayor, with billionaire and part-time Hill Country resident George Strait, even with the governor.

"I like what you've done with the place."

"You know how it is—my work is in the field, not in here."

Which was an acceptable way of saying

Bannister liked to be seen. Someone else could take care of the paperwork.

Tony nodded as if he agreed and jumped right in. "How are you going to rule Dixon's death?"

"I don't make that ruling. The ME does. You know that. Or maybe retirement has softened your brain a little."

"What's Millican found?"

"Wish I could share that with you, but an ME's finding is confidential until—"

"Stop." Tony held up his hand like a traffic cop. He'd never been a particularly tactful person, but he'd been a good cop and folks said he was a great detective. He didn't have the time or patience for whatever game Bannister felt like playing, and he certainly didn't have time to stroke the man's ego.

"Agatha is my neighbor, and—"

"I noticed you two seemed pretty cozy."

Bannister was about to say more. He was about to say something they'd both regret because Tony had no problem putting the man in his place even if it meant a physical altercation. He hadn't done much in his retirement but he had stayed in shape, and if there was one thing he never backed away from it was a fight. He didn't see the point. If someone wanted to start something, they were going to do it. Best to meet it head-on.

Somehow, he conveyed all of that to Bannister in a look, because the man backed down, popped a large piece of a bran muffin in his mouth, and swigged it down with coffee.

"Is the case open or closed?"

"It's open, and that's all I can say at the moment."

Which was all he needed to hear. Tony stood up to go, but Bannister wasn't finished.

"What can you tell me about Agatha Lapp?"

"What do you want to know?"

"Her history. I know she's Amish. Those people are all over the area now, and I have to say I don't get it. Seems suspicious to me."

"Which part? The going to church or the helping their neighbor?"

"You thinking of converting?"

Tony balled his hand into a fist. Maybe he was looking for a fight. Maybe it would help to punch something or someone. But instead of giving Bannister the satisfaction, he said, "If you're going to rule Dixon's death a homicide, and if you're looking Agatha's direction…then you're wasting your time."

As Tony left the building, nodding and saying hello to a few of the people he actually liked, he realized he hadn't stopped by because he thought Bannister would share information. He'd come to confirm a hunch, and Jimmy Bannister had done just that.

Russell Dixon's death was not from natural causes.

Driving out of the parking lot, he discovered he wasn't surprised. Something hadn't sat right with him about Agatha's memories. Well, several things actually. And what he'd heard of the witness's testimonies didn't jibe either.

He pulled through the donut shop drive-thru, placed his order, and headed out of town. His place was only two miles west of Hunt, but those two miles made all the difference. The traffic—if you could call four trucks at the red light *traffic*—vanished.

He stopped twice. Though it was early, he knew both the people he needed to speak with would be up, and they were.

By the time he resumed the trek toward home, the clock was edging toward eight. With any luck, Agatha would have fed her guests and have a few moments to talk.

The Guadalupe River sparkled on his left as the sun made a proper show of itself. This truly was a beautiful place to live. His parents would have loved it. And his nephews, well, he'd been saying for over a year now he'd have them out to fish. Why had he put it off?

As he pulled into his driveway, he felt like a man waking from a dream. He didn't know what had happened at Agatha's, but he meant to find out.

He walked next door, but before he could knock Agatha was there, encouraging him to come inside.

Tony followed her into the kitchen. The place smelled wonderful, causing his stomach to growl. Dishes were stacked in the drainer. The table and counters had already been wiped down. Agatha looked as fresh as the summer day outside the window.

"Everyone gone?"

"Oh, *ya*. They go out to play early, but then they're back here napping or reading by the time two o'clock rolls around."

"It's a good spot for a vacation."

"It is indeed."

Tony rattled the bag. "Brought you something."

"That looks like a donut bag."

"It is."

"I bake."

"I know you do." Tony pushed the bag into her hands. "Camilla was one of the best cooks in the county, but she still liked to eat out or have me bring her something from Donut Palace."

"Your wife?"

Tony nodded.

"Sounds like my kind of gal. I baked cinnamon rolls for breakfast. Served them with scrambled eggs, bacon, and a giant bowl of fruit...but there's not much time to eat when you're waiting on guests."

Five minutes later they both had cups of coffee and were sitting outside on the patio situated halfway down the slope of Agatha's back yard. She peeked into the bag. "Hmmm. Can't decide. I love cake with chocolate icing, but the sugar cinnamon looks *gut*, too."

"Take them both, and I'll have the twist and pink candied."

As she divided up the goodies, he glanced around the patio. The area had been leveled and covered with small pea gravel. There were three two-person wrought iron tables and bright, clean cushions. Flowers overflowed the pots situated along the edge of the area, and a knee-high water fountain gurgled from the middle of a bed of ferns. Even as he watched, a male and female cardinal hopped onto the edge of the fountain to drink. Solar powered lights lined the path, and when he looked more closely he saw that the pump on the fountain had a solar panel as well.

"You've done a really nice job here."

"*Danki.*"

"That means…"

"Thank you."

"Ahh…I should have been able to deduce that."

"Since you were apparently a detective."

"Guilty as charged."

It surprised him that it was so easy to banter with her—maybe because he knew she wouldn't misconstrue anything he said. He doubted Agatha had any intention of looking for a man; and if she did, she wouldn't pick a person like himself, a person outside her faith. Raised in the Catholic tradition, Tony understood how much faith and tradition meant in a marriage.

"But seriously. You've made a lot of improvements to the place. How long have you been here?"

"Moved in last August. Texas was having a heat wave and the temps were…"

"Near 100. I remember. Not uncommon for much of the state, but here we usually hover in the 90s."

"I'll admit it crossed my mind that I'd made a huge mistake." She broke the cake donut into four pieces and popped one into her mouth.

"But you like it here?"

"I do. I don't miss the snow one bit."

"Where did you live before?"

"Indiana—Shipshewana. Lots of Amish folks there."

"There were Amish folks who lived here before you."

"My youngest *bruder*—Samuel—and his wife Deborah. They were killed in a buggy accident."

He didn't answer immediately. He was remembering an article in the paper. Camilla had been in the most difficult part of her cancer then, and he barely knew what was going on outside their window. But he did remember the photo of the buggy and the horse and the young driver who'd caused the accident.

"I'm truly sorry for your loss."

She stared down at her hands a second, then met his gaze. "Their life was complete."

Tony started to ask what she meant by that, but it wasn't relevant to the current case. So instead he finished his donuts, then sat back cradling his cup of coffee. "We need to talk about Russell Dixon."

✳

was coming along.

"Exactly," she said.

"So tell me how this works...how do you adhere to the rules of your faith and still run a business?"

"That's the key. It's a business, and our bishop makes allowances for that."

"Give me an example."

"All right." She sat back, more relaxed than when the conversation had first turned toward Russell Dixon. Maybe that was what Tony was doing—trying to loosen her up before he focused more directly on the subject of her deceased guest.

"As Amish, we don't use electricity, computers, many conveniences of the modern world within our homes. For example, I have a horse and buggy instead of a car."

"But I've seen you ride in a car. The other day an Uber driver picked you up."

"I had an appointment over in Kerrville, which is too far to take Doc."

"Doc?"

"My mare."

"So you won't own a car, but you'll ride in one."

"We prefer not to have the expense or convenience of a car."

"Explain that to me."

"When you have a car, you're likely to zip

around for any reason at all. When you have to harness a horse to a buggy, you consolidate your trips. By travelling in the old style, we keep our lives simple and our focus on what matters—home and family. But we don't believe cars are evil."

"Got it. And the electricity and computers?"

"Pretty much the same idea. My cabins have electricity and Wi-Fi for guests. In the house, the suites do not have electricity, and those are the rooms my Amish guests usually book."

"I thought the Coopers were staying in the house."

"They are. The cabins were full." Agatha ate the last bit of her donut, then added, "And the Fishers, who are obviously Amish, are staying in a cabin. Exceptions to our *Ordnung* are allowed on vacation, and they preferred being closer to the river."

"Do you use a computer for business, and do you have a phone?"

"I don't have a cell phone, but I have an office where I have both a telephone landline and a computer...it's handy for taking reservations." She sighed and looked out over the water. "Some Amish would not approve of that. They feel that any electricity in your home is wrong. Other communities allow solar power in the homes— which is what I have here in the main house. The cabins, they're powered with traditional electricity. It all depends on the *Ordnung* of the community."

"And what is that?"

"Our rules or guidelines for living a faithful life."

"Okay. Thank you for explaining that."

"Is it important?"

"It might be. It's hard to say what is and isn't important in an investigation." Tony pushed his coffee cup aside and crossed his arms on the table, making certain he had her complete attention before he continued. "I went into the police department this morning and spoke with Bannister. He wasn't very forthcoming."

"He doesn't want you solving his case."

"Right. It's his turf, and he wants me to respect the very obvious line he's drawn between police and civilians. I'm now a civilian."

"You two worked together before?"

"Yes, before I retired—that was four years ago."

"I heard you call him lieutenant. And you were a detective?"

"Lieutenant is his rank. The highest I rose to was sergeant, which was fine. I never wanted to do the administrative stuff. And yes, I was a detective, as is he."

"Which means you handled murders?"

"Detectives are essentially investigators—they gather facts and collect evidence in many different types of cases."

"All right. You certainly understand more

about these matters than I do." Agatha's anxiety had calmed as Tony spoke. It helped to understand the lay of the land, as her *dat* used to say. "What did you learn when you visited him this morning?"

"Bannister told me the case is still open, which probably means they're going to rule it as a death by unnatural causes."

"Someone killed Mr. Dixon?"

"Maybe, though that category can also include accidents and drug overdoses."

Agatha massaged her left thumb with her right hand. Long ago, when she'd been a young woman, she had the terrible habit of biting her nails. She'd overcome that by substituting something more hygienic.

"I stopped by Julia Perez's home after I'd seen Bannister."

"She's someone you trust?"

"She is. Julia was my secretary long before she worked for Jimmy Bannister, and she's a good person. She wouldn't lie to me. If she felt like she couldn't discuss a thing, she'd say as much, but she wouldn't lie."

"And what did Julia tell you?"

"That the police didn't find Mr. Dixon's phone or computer."

"Well, he definitely had a phone."

"What did it look like?"

"A phone."

Bannister had stopped in front of Agatha. "Agatha Lapp, we are detaining you for questioning in the death of Russell Dixon."

"You can't be serious," Tony muttered.

"I don't understand." Agatha stepped backwards when Bannister reached out to guide her toward the waiting cruisers. "Am I under arrest? Do you think I killed that man?"

Bannister stepped closer and lowered his voice. "Do you really want to do this in front of your guests?"

It was at that moment that both Agatha and Tony looked around. The Glicks and the Fishers had appeared from their morning stroll. Now they were frozen on the path, staring, open-mouthed, at the officer and Agatha.

"I can't...I can't just leave everyone."

"You don't really have a choice," Bannister practically growled.

Tony sighed. He knew there was no use arguing with Bannister, though the man was plainly a fool.

"Can't you just ask me your questions here?"

"I'm afraid it's more serious than that."

"More serious in what way?"

"You can come with us now or I can come back with an arrest warrant this afternoon. It looks better if you cooperate."

Tony couldn't hold himself back a moment longer. He inserted himself between Agatha and

Bannister, lowered his voice so the guests wouldn't hear, and lambasted the man. "You and I both know Agatha didn't kill anyone. Just because you want another notch on your belt—"

"Stay out of this, Vargas."

"A quick arrest looks good until the judge figures out you arrested the wrong person."

"You're lucky I'm not pulling you in with her." Bannister seemed to have forgotten Agatha for a moment. He stood toe to toe with Tony and hissed, "You two obviously have a special relationship. Who's to say you're not involved?"

"A better question is if you're qualified to work in law enforcement."

Bannister spun away from Tony and addressed Agatha. "Mrs. Lapp, you need to come with me."

"All right."

Tony was at Agatha's side in a second. "Don't say a word until your lawyer arrives."

"But—"

"Just promise me you'll wait until your lawyer arrives."

"I don't have a lawyer."

"I'll take care of that."

"Okay." Agatha's hand flew to the top of her head, as if she needed to be sure her head covering was firmly in place. "Can I...get my purse?"

"Go with her, Tami." Bannister turned and strode back to his cruiser without another word.

Tami and Agatha hurried toward the back door, Tony close on their heels.

Once they entered her house, Agatha seemed to recover her equilibrium. She strode to her office, snagged her purse off the back of the door where it was hanging from a hook, and looked longingly at a bag sitting next to a rocking chair.

"Do you think I could take my knitting?"

"No. They won't let you have that."

"Oh."

Tony moved in front of her, ignoring the fact that Tami was sticking close. No doubt she'd been told to listen carefully to anything they said.

"It's going to be all right, Agatha."

"Of course it is. I didn't do anything wrong."

"We're going to straighten this out. I'll call Kiara—Kiara Bledsoe. She's a good person and a fine lawyer. You can trust her."

"Do you really think that's necessary?"

"Wait for her to get there. Don't answer anything until she's in the room with you."

"All right."

"Bannister will figure out he has the wrong person. He's not a bad cop, just overly ambitious." He shot a dark look toward Tami when he said the last, but she only shrugged, her hand resting on the butt of her pistol as if they were two dangerous criminals who might make a break for it at any minute.

"What else can I do here...to help with your guests?"

"Gina should arrive in the next half hour. Ask her to stay until I'm back." Agatha sighed. "I already had a long list of things to do today. One just never knows what direction a day is going to take."

With her head held high, she turned and marched out of the room.

Tony wanted to go with her, but he knew Bannister wouldn't let him in the interrogation room. No, he needed to call Kiara. They'd been through plenty together, and he knew she'd be able to guide Agatha through this.

If she was in town.

If she had time to take on one more case.

If not, she'd recommend someone else highly qualified.

Finding adequate representation for Agatha wasn't the problem.

The problem was that Bannister had unearthed something new regarding the case, and whatever it was must have pointed toward Agatha being the killer.

Chapter Nine

FORTUNATELY, AGATHA was good at waiting. Their church services ran to three hours as they sat on wooden benches with no back support. Sitting in Lieutenant Bannister's interrogation room was not a problem. She only wished she could be knitting.

The clock on the wall inched toward two in the afternoon. At least they'd brought her a bottle of water. She'd spent the first hour praying, the second hour wondering why she was there, and the third thinking of how she could remove the built-up wax from the linoleum floor. The starkness of the room didn't particularly bother her. A table, two chairs on each side. Walls painted a soft gray with a black baseboard.

She'd once stopped by Gina's home when

her friend was watching some detective show on the television. That room was stark looking with cracked linoleum, a stainless steel table, and grimy walls. This room looked quite different from the one portrayed on the program, except for the long, darkened window on the opposite wall. One exactly like that had been in the television show. She understood that she couldn't see through the window, but someone could be watching her. She was tempted to wave at whomever might be sitting on the opposite side.

Despite the built-up wax on the floor, the building itself seemed to be newly constructed. The table had a nice, light, oak veneer finish. The chairs were covered with dark blue upholstery. Industrial-type carpet with a blue and gray pattern softened the sound of footsteps in the hall. She wondered why this interrogation room wasn't carpeted and decided she'd rather not know.

There was a television mounted on the wall, but it was turned off. Perhaps they used it to show criminals their dastardly deeds caught on video. Well, they wouldn't need it for her. Agatha had committed no dastardly deeds. She'd done nothing wrong, and she didn't think she'd ever been videotaped.

She was, however, ready to go home. The fluorescent lights were giving her a headache, her stomach had begun to growl, and any possibility of attacking her to-do list seemed to be vanishing with each minute ticked off the clock. She'd planned to spend an hour working in her vegetable garden, and her guests—if she still had any after they'd watched her escorted away in the police cruiser—would be wondering what had happened to her.

She was seriously considering tapping on the window and telling them she would answer their questions without the lawyer Tony was sending. Why did she need a lawyer? Innocent people didn't need someone to defend them. Did they?

The question had no sooner popped into her head than Tami, the nice police officer who'd driven her to the police station, walked in, followed by a woman Agatha could only assume was the lawyer. Bannister came in last and shut the door behind him.

The woman she didn't know walked around to Agatha's side of the table and set a black leather bag down on the floor as she took a seat. She was slim, well-dressed, middle-aged, and black.

"I'm Kiara Bledsoe." Making no attempt to lower her voice, she added, "Tony sent me. Just follow my lead, and we'll have you out of here in no time."

"I wouldn't be so sure about that, Ms. Bledsoe." Bannister was smiling as if he'd just caught a record-setting fish. "Nice of you to show up for a client you never met, but your overconfidence won't help in this case."

Instead of responding to the bait, Kiara pulled a phone from her purse, tapped the screen a few times, then placed the device in the middle of the table.

"The date is Thursday, June thirteenth, and the time is two seventeen in the afternoon. This questioning is taking place in the Hunt County Sheriff's Department building. My name is Kiara Bledsoe, Esquire, and I am representing Agatha Lapp. Also present for this interrogation are..."

She waited. Bannister had crossed his arms and was shooting darts with his glare, but it didn't intimidate Kiara one bit.

Agatha thought she was going to like this woman.

Finally, Bannister sat up straighter, smoothed down his tie, and said, "Lieutenant James Bannister."

Kiara glanced at the woman sitting beside Bannister.

"Officer Tami Griffin."

Kiara made eye contact with Agatha and nodded her head toward the phone.

"Yes. Of course. My name is Agatha Lapp."

Kiara sat back and smiled, "Let's do this."

Oh, Agatha liked Kiara Bledsoe, Esquire. She'd obviously done this before, probably in this very room, and definitely opposite Bannister. In fact, if Agatha was reading the dynamics between them correctly—and she was exceptionally good at

stabbed a bulleted item and spun the sheet around to face Agatha.

She peered at the sheet, wishing she'd brought her reading glasses. For a moment she leaned closer as if she was missing something, and finally sat back. "What am I looking at?"

"Documentation of your brother's accident—the one that killed him and your sister-in-law."

"I don't understand."

Kiara frowned at the sheet. "What is this, Detective Bannister, and what does it have to do with the matter at hand?"

"I'll tell you what this is—it's motive."

"Motive?" Kiara and Agatha spoke in unison.

"This document, which we found in Dixon's briefcase, states that he was employed to investigate the accident that resulted in the death of Samuel and Deborah Lapp—your brother and sister-in-law. It was his job to assess whether a civil suit brought by the deceased's family had any chance. His conclusion was that no compensation would be due."

"According to this, the woman ran into the back of a buggy." Kiara tapped a well-manicured finger against the form. "Why would benefits be denied?"

Agatha didn't wait for Bannister to answer. "First of all, I never filed a claim. I was told by someone that it might be something I'd want to pursue."

"Told by whom?" Kiara asked.

90

"I don't remember. Someone in a uniform. It was unimportant, as I'm Amish and we don't believe in bringing suit against another person."

"So you say." Bannister sat back and crossed his arms.

Agatha had an intense desire to hand him a dish towel so he could wipe the smug look off his face.

"You were notified of the findings, which is common practice to avoid needless litigation." Bannister nodded toward the sheet. "At the bottom of the form, it lists that this report was copied and mailed to Agatha Lapp."

Agatha had tried not to dwell on that dreadful time. She still missed Samuel and Deborah terribly. It was the one and only reason she'd moved to Texas, to honor what they'd tried to do. At times the grief of their deaths still threatened to weigh her down. She knew they were in a better place and believed she would see them again, but oh, how she missed them.

"Samuel hadn't found the time to add fluorescent triangles on the back of his buggy. They're not allowed in all communities, though more and more are understanding the necessity. Our Amish community here does more than allow the triangles. They encourage and even insist that members have the reflectors, but Samuel...I suppose he'd forgotten."

"So the claim was denied?" Kiara had pulled the paper toward her and was scanning it from top to bottom.

"There never was a claim." Agatha still couldn't imagine what this had to do with a dead guest in Cabin 3.

"And yet the accident was investigated and the possibility of a claim nipped in the bud by Russell Dixon."

"This proves nothing, Bannister." Kiara pushed the form back across the table.

Griffin pulled out another sheet of paper, this time without any prompting from Bannister. "This is a copy of the final risk assessment. Note the beneficiary—Agatha Lapp. Mrs. Lapp, you stood to receive two hundred and fifty thousand dollars if the wrongful death case did go forward. Quite a windfall for someone who claims to live a plain and simple life."

Agatha understood now where this was going. It was a set up. Bannister was ambitious like Tony had warned her. But the fact that Dixon had investigated any potential future claim didn't make her guilty of murder.

She sat back and crossed her arms over her chest.

"I didn't realize Mr. Dixon was involved in investigating the accident, and I never attempted to submit a claim."

"You must have been angry," Bannister prodded.

"I was grieving. There's a difference."

Bannister's voice took on a conciliatory tone, but his body posture still screamed *arrogant jerk*. He propped his elbows on the table, tapped his fingertips together and spoke slowly—as if the truth of what he was saying pained him greatly. "His Bed-and-Breakfast was apparently in quite a state of disrepair. That must have been a disappointment. No doubt you didn't count on having to take a loan out at the bank simply to get the business up and running. Two hundred and fifty thousand dollars would have come in handy, but Russell Dixon stood in the way of you and that money."

"I wasn't looking to make money off my family's tragic death, and you should be ashamed of yourself for suggesting such a thing."

Bannister sat back, apparently surprised that she would shame him.

"I plan to do more than suggest. I plan to arrest you for the murder of Russell Dixon."

Kiara didn't hesitate for even a second. "Has the ME established that Mr. Dixon was, in fact, murdered?" She wasn't easily intimidated, and somehow her strength and resolve fueled Agatha's.

"What we've established is that Mr. Dixon had a deadly peanut allergy, which he put on his reservation form, and don't say you didn't know..."

Griffin handed him yet another sheet of paper.

"There was also a print-out of his reservation in his briefcase. This is a copy, and I'll draw your attention to the highlighted portion."

"I was aware of Mr. Dixon's allergy, which is why I was careful to follow his dietary requests for all of his meals."

"Then explain to me why our lab found peanuts in the half-eaten muffin on his breakfast tray."

Agatha suddenly felt as if she were in an *Englisch* movie with too much information coming at her too fast. Bannister was talking nonsense, and she'd learned long ago that if you argue with a fool, both of you look stupid. She settled for stating the obvious. "I can't explain that."

"What did you do with his EpiPen?"

"Excuse me?"

"Every person with a life-threatening allergy carries an EpiPen on them at all times. What did you do with Dixon's?"

"I didn't do anything with it. I never saw it."

"Did you sneak into his cabin and steal it?"

"*Nein.*"

"A warrant was issued by a judge early this morning. I have a crew at your home right now, looking for the pen as well as any other evidence. We'll find what we need, and when we do we will arrest you for the murder of Russell Dixon."

Agatha felt as if the room were beginning to

spin. The thought occurred to her that she needed some fresh air, and then she had a vision of herself in prison, behind bars, where fresh air would be a distant memory.

"We're done here." Kiara pushed the sheets of paper back across the table toward Dixon. "You can keep those, and let me know when you have actual charges to bring against my client."

Snatching her leather bag off the floor, Kiara scooped up her phone, tapped the off button, and escorted Agatha out of the room.

he hadn't yet identified, that was important to him.

Five minutes later they were sitting in the corner booth at Sammi's, sunlight pouring through the windows, steaming cups of coffee in front of them, and lunch on the way.

Kiara caught Tony up while Agatha stared out the window.

"Good," Tony said. When both women stared at him in surprise, he added, "It sounds to me like Bannister showed all his cards. As long as we know his game plan, we know what our defense needs to look like."

"What makes you think he showed all his cards?" Kiara asked.

"Jimmy Bannister is a lot of things—motivated, intelligent, ambitious..." He downed half the coffee in his mug, frowned, and added another packet of sugar. "What he's not, is calculating. He's never been the kind of guy to hold his cards close to his chest. Whatever evidence he felt he'd discovered, he threw at you this morning."

"No holding back?"

"He never has. He's been this way since I've known him, since I started working with him."

Agatha pulled her attention away from the window. "You worked with him?"

"Sure, and he always wanted to use a frontal attack. It made him crazy when I'd insist on holding something back in a case. He thinks if you dump everything on a suspect at once, they'll disintegrate before your eyes and confess."

"Agatha definitely did not disintegrate."

"Which reminds me." Agatha smiled at Kiara. "*Danki* for coming simply because Tony called you."

"I'll let you in on a secret...I owe Tony a few favors. Quite a few. This doesn't begin to cover it."

Tony laughed out loud. When he saw the look of surprise on Agatha's face, he added, "I'll explain later. No doubt Kiara has a full slate today."

"I do, but we need to go over a few things." She pulled out a tablet—yellow paper and black lines—and started listing items. "Bannister is correct that he has motive."

"I honestly didn't know Mr. Dixon was even involved in my *bruder*'s case. If I'd seen the name before, I'd forgotten it."

"He can't prove you remembered who Dixon was, and you can't prove you didn't. Everything else being equal, it's enough to establish motive."

"And the muffins?" Tony asked.

"Again, he can't prove Agatha made them. It doesn't stand as evidence against her unless he has her fingerprints on them..."

"I don't understand that part. I might have forgotten a name on a form from a year ago, but I don't forget my guests dietary requests. I very specifically made sure everything I made this weekend was peanut free. It's easier than making separate food for one guest."

Tony exchanged a knowing look with Kiara.

"What?" Agatha asked.

"Only what you've probably already figured out." Kiara tapped her pen against the pad of paper. "If you didn't put peanuts in his breakfast muffins..."

"I didn't. And I also didn't steal his EpiPen. I don't even know what one looks like."

"Then someone else did." Kiara resumed writing on the tablet. "Who else had access to the cabins? Did someone see another person near Dixon's cabin?"

"Jasmine claimed to have seen him arguing with the Cox brothers." Tony gave Kiara a summarized version of what Jasmine had related to Agatha.

"Did he have other enemies? Had there been threats against him?"

She waited a moment and when no one had anything else to add to her list, she capped her pen and put everything back in her bag. The waitress deposited their lunch on the table—a club sandwich for Agatha, a chef salad for Kiara, and eggs with tortillas, hot sauce, and possibly the kitchen sink for Tony.

"A new case always did make me hungry," he explained before digging in.

As they ate, they spoke of other things.

Agatha learned that Kiara lived in one of the new condos farther down the river from her place, she'd been in business for ten years, and she had a full case load.

"Are you sure you have time to take on my case?"

"I'll make time."

When they finished eating, Tony tossed several bills down on the table. As they stood outside in the sunshine, next to Tony's pickup truck and Kiara's bright yellow Jeep, Agatha reached into her purse and pulled out her wallet. "We didn't talk about how much I owe you."

"Nothing, for the moment. This morning was all my pleasure." Promising she'd be in touch, Kiara climbed into the vehicle, music pouring out of it as soon as she started the engine, and waved as she pulled out onto the county road.

Tony was driving them toward home when Agatha sighed, turned to him, and said, "She seems to be good at what she does."

"Kiara is the best, but more importantly, she's one of the good ones."

"What do you mean?"

"It's one thing to be a good lawyer, which she is. But it's another thing to fight for what's right, for the innocent. If Kiara's convinced you're innocent, she'll move mountains to convince a judge of the same."

Chapter Twelve

AGATHA HADN'T realized she'd missed lunch and actually eaten dinner with Tony and Kiara. She still wasn't quite used to the long Texas days, and the hours she'd spent inside the Hunt Police Department offices hadn't helped. She was surprised to climb the steps of her porch, walk into the kitchen, and find Gina doing the dinner dishes.

"Are you hungry?"

"Just ate."

"Good. I was hoping you weren't a guest of the Hunt PD this entire time."

Gina was fort-nine years old, didn't bother to dye her short black hair that was shot through with gray, and had the body of a long-distance runner. She wasn't a long distance runner. She'd never participated in athletics of any sort. She'd shared all that when she'd shown up in answer to Agatha's ad for help the previous fall. They'd become close friends almost immediately.

Perhaps that was because they were both single women.

Perhaps it was because they'd both passed the midlife crisis age.

Possibly it was because they'd both suffered a fair amount of tragedy in the past.

Or maybe it was because *Gotte* had seen that Agatha needed a sympathetic soul in her life, someone who could bridge the gap that existed between the Amish world and the *Englisch* one. Gina did all of that and more.

"Sit down and I'll make you some tea."

"I've been sitting all day. I'm exhausted and full of energy at the same time."

"How about we go out and check your garden, then. I haven't had time, what with Bannister's men stomping through the house, turning things inside out and taking whatever they pleased."

Agatha peeked from the kitchen into her office, but it looked exactly as she'd left it.

"I put everything back and cleaned off the finger print powder—as if they'd need that to prove you'd been in your own office. That group reminded me of McGruff the Crime Dog—basically harmless but leaves a lot of work in his wake."

Gina marched toward the back porch, assuming Agatha would follow, which she did. An hour outside sounded like just what the doctor would order if she'd gone to him and said, "I feel all catawampus. What do you recommend?"

Thirty minutes later, they'd run the green bean shoots up the trellises, threaded new tomato growth through the cages, and pulled a few weeds. Agatha's apron was dirty, she had soil beneath her nails, and hair was escaping from her *kapp*. She felt immeasurably better. As they worked, she'd caught Gina up on all that had transpired. Now they sat on a bench she'd positioned at the end of the long garden rows. The bench afforded a nice view of the river.

"I should go check on my guests."

"If they needed you right now, you'd know."

"I suppose."

They fell into a comfortable silence, broken a few minutes later by Gina exclaiming, "This is a real mess. And I don't need to point out that it comes at the worst possible time."

"Thanks for pointing that out."

"Only voicing what you're thinking."

"Exactly."

"Your business is just beginning to grow. You had another half dozen reservations made on-line today."

"I did?"

"You're nearly booked through the fall."

"Definitely a good thing."

"Unless Bannister arrests you. I can't run this place by myself."

"You probably could."

"The sign out front plainly says Agatha's Amish Bed-and-Breakfast."

"True."

"And I don't know how to look after your horse."

"I think we're off topic here."

They sighed at the same moment, glanced sideways at one another, and started laughing. Perhaps it was all the pent-up energy or the emotional highs and lows of the day, but Agatha laughed until tears streamed down her face.

Finally she wiped her eyes with the sleeve of her dress. "Sorry. I was just imagining you driving a buggy."

"Or wearing one of those bonnets."

"Or living in a house with no television."

The Beilers walked past and waved at Agatha as if it had been a completely normal day.

Both Agatha and Gina stood to walk back to the house, but Agatha detoured to walk closer to the pasture and offer a carrot to her horse. She'd need to come out later and fill her oat bucket, maybe give her a rub down, but first she needed to check on each of her guests. She had turned back toward Gina and was walking back toward her when she noticed Fonzi lying up against the barn, and beside him...

She stopped and squatted, trying to make sense of what she was seeing.

"What are you staring at?"

"Come and look at this."

It was a large, man-sized boot print. From the position of the print it looked as if someone had been standing with their back to the barn.

"There hasn't been any rain," Gina said. "Why is there a boot print?"

"We installed those automatic sprinklers a few weeks ago. Remember? That nice young boy from Kerrville came over and did it for me. Works off solar energy, so the bishop allowed it."

"Okay. So could it be his foot print?"

"*Nein*. That was two weeks ago, and this looks like a fresh print to me."

"So you're a tracker now?"

"I can't imagine a guest standing here against the barn. Not when there's a perfectly good bench over there."

"It's only a boot print, Agatha. I doubt this case is going to turn on that."

"According to Tony, cases can turn on a dime."

"Far be it from me to argue with the good detective, though you do realize the man has been hiding in his house the past couple of years? It could be that he's gone a little..." She twirled a finger next to her head.

"*Narrisch?*"

"Whatever." Gina pulled a cell phone out of her back jeans pocket and snapped a photo of the boot print. "I guess it couldn't hurt to show him the picture. If he thinks it's important, he can come over and case the area."

They walked back to the house in silence and stopped at the steps to the back porch. Both women proceeded to stomp dirt off their shoes. Agatha glanced at her friend, but didn't ask what was on her mind. Sometimes, especially with Gina, it was best to wait. With her eyes squinting and her bottom lip pulled in between her teeth she looked as if she were readying for a fight. Finally, she turned to Agatha and shared what had obviously been bothering her all along.

"Someone's targeting you."

"What do you mean?"

"I mean, someone killed Dixon. Someone knew about his allergy, snuck into his room, stole his EpiPen, then later swapped out the breakfast you left on the front porch, leaving a muffin filled with peanuts."

"Why would anyone do that?"

"I have no idea, but when we figure out the answer to that question, we'll be a whole lot closer to finding out who the real murderer is."

Chapter Thirteen

TONY WAITED a few hours. He wanted Agatha to have time to put her house back together and attend to her guests. He knew she was still awake because he could see her sitting with the Willis family on the porch. The solar-powered lights mounted to the porch railing gave off a soft light.

When Tony called out and climbed the steps, Stuart and Brooklyn stood as if to go. Stuart was holding baby Hudson, who waved a small hand excitedly in the air and giggled. Brooklyn, as usual, had her camera hanging from a strap around her neck. Tony wondered if she was a professional photographer or if snapping pictures was merely a hobby.

"Don't leave on my account," Tony said.

"Probably you two have things to talk about."

"We do, but actually I'd like to ask you a few questions about what you said in your statement."

Brooklyn looked uneasily at Stuart. They seemed to decide at the same moment that staying would be the wiser thing to do. Both sat back down on the porch swing. "There's really not much else we can add," Stuart said.

"That's all right. Just talk me through it."

So they did. Brooklyn again explained about the baby cutting teeth, waking in the middle of the night, and deciding that perhaps a bottle would quiet him. "I came down the stairs and into the kitchen. I guess I surprised him."

"Why do you say that?"

"He jumped, looked startled like he'd been caught doing something he shouldn't."

"And you shared all this with the police?"

"Yes, she did." Stuart scooted closer to his wife. "I honestly don't see the point in going over it again."

Instead of addressing that, Tony turned his attention back to Brooklyn. "And you're sure it was Mr. Dixon?"

"Why would I lie about that?" Brooklyn's gaze darted toward Stuart, who had put an arm around her shoulders as if he needed to protect her.

"I wasn't suggesting that you were lying—"

"My wife was trying to be helpful." Stuart stood

and shifted baby Hudson to his other arm. Brooklyn joined him and they huddled there, looking ready to stand together against the world.

"And I was only suggesting that it might be hard to discern who she saw given the darkness in the kitchen and the hour."

"I know who I saw." Brooklyn raised her chin an inch.

"What do you think he was doing?"

"How should I know? He came out of the pantry. For all I know he was looking for something to eat."

Agatha cleared her throat even as she shook her head. "I keep fresh snacks on the counter with a sign saying *Help yourself*, so that's not likely."

"I trust you don't have any more questions, or if you do—check with that Lieutenant Bannister and read our statement. Now if you'll excuse us, it's been a long day." Stuart cupped his wife's elbow and turned her toward the front door.

Tony watched in surprise as they walked into the house.

"Are they always like that?"

"Like what?"

"Prickly."

Agatha smiled. "You Texans have funny expressions, but I get it. Prickly—like a cactus."

"Surely you've heard someone called prickly before."

"*Nein.*"

"How would an Amish person describe them?"

"My *mamm* would spout a proverb."

"Such as?"

"You can look a man into the face but not into the heart."

"That's a good one, and it might apply to the Willis family."

Agatha set her chair to rocking. "I don't know. They seem like a nice couple, only terribly young."

"I've noticed that my perception of age changes the older I get."

"*Ya,* there was a time I thought forty was awfully old. Now I've turned fifty-five, but in my heart I still feel like a *youngie* some days."

"Mind if we go inside and check out the pantry?"

"Not at all."

Five minutes later, they'd scoured the small walk-in closet from floor to ceiling.

"Can't imagine what he might have been after." Agatha worried the string to her prayer *kapp.*

"Nothing stored here except food and drinks."

"Which are on the counter and in the fridge."

"The breaker box is here." Tony stepped closer and stared at the box. Pulling his pen out of his pocket, he pried the door open.

"Why the pen?"

"Because Bannister might want to come back

and check this for fingerprints."

"I don't understand."

Tony didn't answer immediately. He wasn't exactly sure how much of what he was thinking he should share with Agatha. After all, at this point, he had no proof. So he shrugged, motioned her back out into the kitchen, and said, "Or it could be nothing. I also wanted to speak with the Coopers. Are they here?"

"*Nein*. They decided to go to dinner and dancing over in Kerrville. Left me a note that they'd be back late."

"I suppose I could come speak with them in the morning." He glanced around the kitchen. Through the window, he could see his place, but for some reason the thought of going back over there and stewing over this case didn't appeal to him at all. "Would you like to go back outside?"

"I would love that. The porch may be my favorite part of this place. It reminds me of home."

They walked outside and Tony sat beside her. It still surprised him how comfortable he felt around Agatha. It had been a long time since he'd enjoyed the company of another person—a long time since he'd let anyone close. During Camilla's illness, he'd pretty much kept people at arm's length. Why had he done that?

Agatha didn't interrupt his musings.

After a few minutes, he told her Gina had sent

him the picture of the boot print, but he didn't see how it could be related. "It's good you're keeping an eye open though."

"I continue to hope this will all...blow away."

"That's not likely."

"I'm aware, but a girl can hope."

Tony waited, unsure exactly what he should say next. Agatha didn't make any effort to jump in and fill the void in the conversation. Silences seemed not to bother her, which after Tony's year of mourning was a relief. He'd grown accustomed to quiet and could think better when he wasn't besotted by voices and music and the sounds of techno gadgets. Instead, all he heard was the sound of crickets, a slight breeze in the trees, and, if he listened closely, the flowing waters of the Guadalupe River.

"I didn't come here only to talk about the case."

"Indeed?"

"I wanted to check on you, Agatha." When she didn't respond to that at all, he sat forward, elbows on his knees and studied her in the dim light. "You've been through a traumatic experience. I know first-hand that these things can be difficult..."

"I feel okay, maybe a bit tired."

"It's not unusual for there to be a delayed reaction."

"Hmmm."

"The symptoms of PTSD include re-experiencing the trauma."

113

"And it wasn't you."

"Indeed."

"Once your guests leave, once they scatter to the wind, it will be harder to figure out who did it. And if we don't figure it out, this will hang over you. It could ruin your reputation."

"I have a *gut* reputation."

"You did, before this. But who wants to book a weekend they might not return from?" Gina finished her cinnamon roll, then wiped nonexistent crumbs onto the plate and carried the plate to the sink. Sitting back down across from Agatha, she looked even more serious than she had when she'd first walked into the room.

"I know you're no Agatha Christie."

Agatha rolled her eyes. She'd heard that joke since she was a *youngie*. Even Amish folks knew of the famous writer.

"And I'm certainly no sleuth like Miss Marple, but we can do this." Gina's gaze flitted around the room, as if she might spy the offending party lurking near the stove or behind the refrigerator. "Think about it. Whoever swapped out Dixon's breakfast had access to this property. The chances that someone who didn't belong here moseyed up to Dixon's porch and changed his breakfast, without anyone noticing, well that's a slim chance indeed."

"I don't know what we can do, Gina. We cooperated with the police, Kiara has promised to represent me if it comes to that, and Tony is helping any way he can."

"Which is all good, but I'm talking about you and me...we are the ones who have the most to lose and we need to solve this."

Her intensity should have made Agatha laugh, but instead, she squirmed under her friend's gaze.

"I don't know how to do that."

"We keep our eyes open. Someone isn't telling the truth."

"Any guesses?"

"Something is up with those Cox brothers."

"They certainly don't seem to be catching any fish."

"Also, I'm not buying the Coopers' story. For some reason, they want to turn our attention to Mason and Paxton."

"Tony didn't believe them either."

"The Willis family seems innocent enough, maybe too innocent. Brooklyn claimed she was downstairs because the baby was teething, but I've been around teething babies all my life and they've never been as good-natured as Hudson."

"Now that you mention it, Hudson smiled at me bright as the sun yesterday morning."

"So why was she downstairs in the middle of the night?"

"Insomnia?"

Gina waved that excuse away. "Then we have

your Amish guests."

"Yes?" Agatha couldn't wait to hear what Gina had to say about the three Amish couples. They were all over sixty and from the northern part of the country. They couldn't possibly have known Russell Dixon.

"I'm not sure. There's something...off about them."

Agatha shrugged. How was she to answer that? Amish often seemed very different to *Englischers*. They were different, but it didn't mean they were killers. In fact, the thought was preposterous. Amish adhered strongly to a policy of non-violence. She just couldn't imagine such a thing.

"We'll both keep our eyes open." Agatha reached across the table and squeezed Gina's hand. "Maybe something will pop up."

"As long as it isn't another dead body."

They both stood and began preparing breakfast for her guests, working seamlessly side by side. Agatha put the uncomfortable conversation behind her and focused on the day ahead—working in her garden, cleaning the guest rooms, and hopefully finding time to finish some knitting.

That peaceful vision was shattered by Gina's final comment on the subject.

"Think about motive, Agatha."

"The killer's motive?"

"Exactly. Someone wants you out of business."

"How did you arrive at that conclusion?" She'd been chopping a russet potato to make hash browns. Her hand paused mid-air, the blade of the knife gleaming in the sunlight. She stared at Gina, who seemed entirely too caught up in all of this.

"Think about it. If you'd been arrested—"

"I wasn't."

"If you're eventually found guilty—"

"I won't be. I'm innocent."

"Then this Bed-and-Breakfast will close. It would have to. I can't run a B&B. Oh, I know I'm useful in the background, but you're the quintessential Amish *mamm*."

"I'm not sure that's a compliment."

"The thing to ask yourself is, who would want to see you go out of business?"

Agatha resumed chopping the potato into small pieces, perhaps a bit too vigorously. "I don't know who killed Mr. Dixon or why they killed him, but one thing I'm sure of is that it had nothing to do with me."

doorway. Agatha was sitting at the table with an older Amish man and woman.

"Tony. I didn't hear you knock." Agatha jumped up and motioned to a chair. "Can I get you some coffee? Tea?"

"No, thank you. I'm good."

"This is my bishop and his *fraa*—Jonas and Minerva Schrock." Agatha glanced at the older couple and then back at Tony. "Tony is my neighbor. He was the police detective with the Hunt Police Department before he retired."

The Schrocks looked at him and smiled, though neither offered to shake his hand. He was learning that shaking hands wasn't a very Amish thing to do.

"I can come back if now isn't a good time."

"Now's perfect. We were just talking about..." Agatha's hand fluttered out and away. "The events of the past two days."

"Real sad about Agatha's guest," Jonas said.

"Mr. Dixon's life was complete," Minerva added. "Still...such a tragedy."

"And for Agatha to be caught up in the middle of it... That's why we stopped by. We wanted to assure her that we're here for her...anything she needs, all she has to do is ask."

Tony had done a little reading about the Amish the night before when he couldn't sleep. He thought he understood what her bishop was saying—if she needed money or someone to look after the place or a friend in the middle of the night, she'd have it. He wondered how different the world would be if everyone had that level of support.

Clearing his throat, he turned his attention to the matter at hand. "That's why I'm here, actually. I'd like to help Agatha."

"It's *gut* that you know the legal system," Minerva said.

Jonas nodded in agreement. "As you can imagine, we don't normally involve ourselves in such matters. Our goal is to remain separate...set apart...even though we may work directly beside *Englischers*."

Tony nodded as though what they were saying made perfect sense, and on one level maybe it did. As a detective, he'd met many people who had a motto of *family first*. For some, it meant that family came first, middle, and last. With his Catholic upbringing, he was well acquainted with the attitude that family was everything. He understood that, in a sense, an Amish community was one large family.

"Agatha has asked me to help her," Tony explained. "Though I have no official position with the police department anymore."

"Tony's wife died nine months ago." She refilled the bishop's coffee cup. "He took early retirement to care for her and spend time with her."

"And I'm so glad I did." Tony cleared his throat. He didn't often talk about Camilla. People who'd never experienced terminal illness with a loved one rarely understood, and those who had been through a similar situation didn't need it explained. "But back to Agatha..."

"Never thought I'd find myself visiting an *Englisch* police station," she admitted.

"Agatha told us what you did for her." Jonas ran his fingers through his salt and pepper beard. "She mentioned that you provided a lawyer who represented her. That was very kind."

"Kiara Bledsoe is a successful attorney with an unblemished reputation. Both our local judges, as well as her fellow attorneys, respect her."

"We have plenty of money in our benevolence fund, and we're more than happy to compensate Ms. Bledsoe on Agatha's behalf."

"At this point no fee is involved." When Jonas and Minerva looked at Tony with brows raised, he clarified, "She owed me a favor. If it comes to a trial she'll charge her standard rate, which is a reasonable one, but hopefully the investigation will move on and Bannister's fascination with Agatha will pass."

Agatha had been standing at the counter with her back against it, watching the three of them talk. At the mention of Bannister, she walked to the table and sat down. "Bannister seemed pretty certain I was involved." She let her gaze drift over each of them, then shrugged.

"He's fishing." Tony pulled out the small

notepad he kept in his shirt pocket. It was a habit from his detective days and one he'd quickly picked back up when he became involved with Dixon's murder. "I'm curious about this situation with your brother and his insurance. If you can explain it to me, maybe I'd understand what Bannister is after. Once we understand that connection, we can convince him to move on to looking for the actual killer."

"So it was murder?" Minerva asked.

"Yes. It's officially been declared a homicide."

He waited and allowed Agatha to gather her thoughts. If the subject affected her emotionally, he couldn't tell. Agatha struck him as the kind of person who carefully considered what to say before she spoke—rare in a person in modern society.

"You have to understand that I wasn't living here when Samuel died. In fact, I hadn't even visited Texas, though of course my *bruder* wrote me letters... or rather, his *fraa* did."

"Samuel was in the first group to come down," Jonas explained. "When we start a new community we try to have ten to twelve families, including one bishop. I was pleased to have Samuel and Deborah in that first group."

"How did he afford this place?" Tony thought the question might offend, and that wasn't his intent, but he needed to know Samuel's background since Bannister seemed to believe his death was tied to Agatha's property. In fact, the only common denominator he could think of between Dixon and Agatha was her brother's death. It seemed wise to trace that particular thread back to the beginning.

"You're going to need a cup of coffee if you want the whole story." Agatha fetched coffee as well as a plate of oatmeal bars.

When was the last time he'd eaten something homemade? Not counting the dinner she sent home with him two nights before, he probably hadn't had anything homemade since Camilla was well enough to cook. Oh, he heated soups and made sandwiches and scrambled eggs, but his cooking skills were limited. He'd forgotten how good homemade food tasted.

Ten minutes later, he understood that Amish did sometimes take out loans for businesses and that Samuel had done that very thing. For a down payment, he used money his family pooled together combined with his own savings. He purchased the land from someone who had specifically wanted to sell to Amish.

"Seems Mrs. Klaassen had kin who were Mennonite." Jonas smiled and slipped a thumb under his suspenders. "She had a deep respect for the Anabaptist faith—which includes both Amish and Mennonite. When she learned we were considering a community here, she offered several pieces of property she owned below the actual value."

"That was more than kind of her. Do you know

her full name?"

"Kathy Klaassen. I've met her on two occasions. She's an older woman with vast resources—seems her husband made a fortune in oil before the prices dropped."

"Does she live here? I've never heard of her."

"She has a place in Ingram and a penthouse in San Antonio. Not that I've ever seen it, but there was an article in the paper a year or so ago."

"All right, so Samuel buys the property with a loan. I seem to remember that he first set it up as a Bed-and-Breakfast. How did he do?"

Jonas and Minerva shared a look, and Agatha stared out the kitchen window.

When no one answered, Tony crossed his arms and sat back. "What aren't you tell me? What am I missing here?"

Chapter Sixteen

AGATHA WANTED to hop up and go work in the garden, or see how the Cox brothers were doing fishing in the river, or even scrub one of the upstairs bathrooms. Anything would be preferable to speaking badly of Samuel. She understood Tony was asking because of his interest in the case. So she stayed where she was, fought to ignore the fluttering in her stomach, and met Tony's confused gaze. "It's no secret, really. My *bruder* wasn't much of a businessman."

"Why do you say that?"

"You lived next door, Tony. Didn't you notice that the lawn was overgrown and the place in general was quite unkempt?"

"Can't say I did." Tony sat back and tapped

his finger against his lips. He finally shook his head. "I wouldn't have known if a circus had moved in next door. My attention was completely focused on Camilla."

"Samuel had a *gut* heart," Jonas said.

"And Deborah was a hard worker." Minerva turned her coffee cup to the left and then the right.

Agatha realized it was up to her to explain Samuel's business failings. Minerva and Jonas wouldn't speak poorly of the dead. "Samuel never quite understood the concept of being an entrepreneur. Jonas tried to counsel with him a few times."

"I did. Each time he listened eagerly and patiently, even taking notes as you're doing. Next time I came by, he'd be down at the river fishing."

"He kept a detailed log of the fish he caught, but the receipts for this place were all stuffed in an old shoebox." Agatha smiled and took a sip from her now cold coffee. "He lived life to its fullest."

Tony waited for more, but Agatha wasn't sure exactly what to say. She summed it up with, "They never had many guests here, and the ones they had didn't return for a second visit. My *bruder* was friendly and Deborah was a *gut* cook, but it takes more than that to run a Bed-and-Breakfast. Guests need to feel like they've stepped into someplace special. That doesn't happen when things need painting or mending."

Tony offered her a weak smile. Finally, he looked down at his list and moved on.

"Tell me about the accident."

"It was raining and the road was slick." Jonas stretched his neck to the left and the right. "We hadn't been here long, then. There weren't any buggy signs up on the roads, though of course people knew we'd moved into the area and that we drove buggies. At least the people who lived close by knew."

"Though we have a lot of visitors in this part of the state," Minerva piped up. "They might not have been aware, and the woman who hit Samuel—she was from the Houston area."

"Samuel was coming back from town. He and Deborah had been to the market. He had a problem with a buggy wheel...or so witnesses told us later. One of our men had even pulled over to help him, but Samuel waved him on. After he fixed the problem, he continued home."

"By then it was quite dark," Minerva said. "And beginning to rain."

"The woman coming around the corner was going the speed limit, but when she tried to stop, the slick roads..." Jonas's hands spread out in front of him. "The emergency personnel said both Deborah and Samuel died instantly."

"Amazingly, the horse survived." Minerva picked at an oatmeal bar, crumbling it into pieces.

"How is that possible?" Tony asked. "That the

horse would survive?"

"There's a break-away bar between the horse and the buggy," Jonas explained. "When the buggy flipped to the right, Doc went left. The bar broke—as it's designed to do under that amount of pressure—and the horse was standing by the side of the road when the police arrived."

"Was the person cited for DUI or DWI?" He'd meant to look that up the night before, but after researching the Amish in general, he'd fallen asleep.

"No. The young woman's tests came back clear of any substances. She sustained injuries as well, and we offered to pay her medical bills."

"Wait. You offered to pay her medical bills?"

"She's a single mom, or so we were told. We're commanded to take care of widows and orphans." Jonas shrugged. "It seemed like the thing to do, but her lawyer advised against her taking the money."

"Okay. So then you filed a wrongful death suit?"

"*Nein.*" Agatha took up the story. "We don't believe in suing."

"She killed two members of your family."

"And she'll be answering to our heavenly Father for that, but it isn't my place to judge her." Agatha raised her eyes to his. "She didn't set out that evening intent on killing Samuel and Deborah. There was no malicious planning on her part. It was all a terrible accident."

"Well..." Tony ran his hand over the top of his head. He'd read that the Amish were forgiving. He'd even read about the West Nickel Mines School shooting. Charles Carl Roberts had shot ten girls in the one-room schoolhouse, killing five. In the immediate aftermath of the tragedy, the local Amish community had cared for the shooter's wife and children.

He'd read the facts, but it hadn't really sunk in just how different the Amish attitude toward tragedy was from mainstream America.

"It's called grace," Jonas said, tapping his fingers against the table. "That's the word you're looking for—grace. We are given grace by our Heavenly Father, and so we offer it to all."

"Don't get him started preaching," Minerva said with a smile.

"So who filed suit?"

Agatha once again took up the story. "The police took the case to the grand jury, who didn't find sufficient cause to indict the woman. Her name was Willow, by the way—Willow Davis. The public defender contacted me, said we might have recourse, pending the results of the insurance investigation. He advised that I hire an independent investigator, but I saw no reason."

"The insurance company would have assumed you were going to do just that." Tony jotted a few notes on his paper, then dropped his pen on top of the pad. "Enter Russell Dixon."

"I looked back over the paperwork last night." Agatha fought to ignore the tightness in her chest. Looking over the details of her bruder's death had been difficult. "Mr. Dixon found that Samuel hadn't added the required triangles to the buggy. He'd meant to, I'm sure, the same as he meant to fix the front porch steps and paint the house."

"Most people would have pursued the case regardless of those facts. Often insurance companies will pay to make a case go away."

"Possibly, but the case died from lack of interest." Jonas glanced at Agatha and then back at Tony. "Agatha didn't want to pursue it. We only hire lawyers when there's no other path, and in this case, it all seemed to be a terrible accident. What good could possibly come from drawing out the process?"

"It wouldn't bring Samuel or Deborah back." Agatha carried her coffee cup to the sink, rinsed it, placed it in the drainer, and turned to look at them. She crossed her arms, then decided that felt too defensive so she dropped them by her side. When had her body started feeling so awkward? It was as if her own arms didn't quite fit her body. "The public defender contacted me, said there could be a substantial amount of money recovered from the woman's insurance company, and suggested I pursue that in the civil courts. I told her I wasn't interested."

"Just like that?"

"Of course. Money—it wouldn't cure the grief in my heart. I even received offers to buy this place, and I considered that. But in the end, it seemed the best way to honor Samuel's life—Samuel's and Deborah's—was to try and see their dream of an Amish Bed and Breakfast along the Guadalupe River become a success."

Tony picked up his pen and tapped it against his note pad. "Russell Dixon had been assigned to the insurance investigation, which meant he worked for either the company or an independent contractor. Sometimes insurance companies want to maintain the illusion of using an uninvolved investigator, but of course they're paid by the company, so the illusion of objectivity is just that."

"I wouldn't know." Agatha stared down at her apron, straightened it, and returned her attention to Tony. "As I said to Lieutenant Bannister, I'd never met Mr. Dixon before he checked into his room earlier this week, and I didn't remember seeing his name on any form."

"So Russell Dixon found that the buggy was out of compliance. He reported back to the insurance company. I'd like to get a copy of that report and see what else he found."

"What's the point?"

"Someone wanted him dead. We need to prove it wasn't you."

"The entire idea is ludicrous. For the sake of argument, say I was angry about Dixon's investigation. How would killing him solve anything? The report had already been filed."

"People kill for different reasons—revenge, passion, even money."

"We're pacifists," Jonas reminded him. "Agatha had no reason to seek revenge. She didn't harbor particularly strong feelings about the case, though no doubt she was grieving the death of Samuel and Deborah. As for the money, she didn't need it."

Tony didn't respond to that immediately. He tucked his notepad and pen back in his pocket and then studied the three people waiting on his reply. "For lack of interest, the case was dropped. Then ten months later Dixon shows up at your Bed-and-Breakfast and is killed."

"How do those two things fit together?" Agatha once again sat down beside him. "Or could it be coincidence?"

"I have no idea," Tony answered honestly. "But we're going to find out, Agatha. One way or another, I promise you that we will figure this thing out. You've been through enough this past year. I'm not going to let Bannister bully you just because he wants another solved case on his resume. One way or another, we're going to find Russell Dixon's killer."

✻

Chapter Seventeen

JONAS AND Minerva left, and Agatha led Tony
outside where the Coopers were once again
resting under the shade of the trees that bordered
the river.

Tony apologized for disturbing them, but
unlike the Willises the night before, neither Jasmine
nor Xavier seemed bothered by his questions.

Jasmine went over what she'd seen in the early
morning hours before the murder.

"And you're sure it was Dixon?"

"I'd seen him leaving his cabin the day before. If
it wasn't the same man, he must have stolen Dixon's
clothes." Jasmine tried to pass if off as a joke.

Tony waited. He didn't laugh or even smile.
He wanted to see if she would add anything else.

Finally, she said, "Yes. I'm sure it was him."

"All right. And Xavier, you told Agatha that you were filling the hydration packs in the bathroom and didn't see anything?"

"Correct."

Tony pulled out a small pad of paper and pretended to stare at the notes. It was a stalling technique. He didn't need to look at notes to see what he'd written on the sheet of paper. Finally, he put his finger on a line of writing and glanced up. "I'm just curious…"

"About?"

"Why you'd need to fill your packs when other guests reported seeing you filling them at the water hose outside, earlier that afternoon when you came back from hiking. Why would you need to fill them again the next morning?"

A flicker of anger passed over Xavier's eyes, flashed so quickly that Tony might have imagined it.

"You got me. Gosh, I guess it's a good thing they're not looking at us for the murder." No one laughed, and Xavier crossed his arms. "You're right. I did fill them the night before. I'd completely forgotten that. But I was still in the bathroom when Jasmine was looking out the window. I was getting ready for the hike."

Xavier and Jasmine exchanged a look, but neither added to the story.

Tony smiled and slapped his pad shut, sticking

it back in his shirt pocket. "I knew there was a logical explanation."

The young couple seemed to relax.

"Xavier isn't used to getting up so early. I'm surprised he can remember what he did at all."

"Plus all this fresh air and sunshine is messing with my brain." He laughed and pulled Jasmine closer to his side, draping his arm around her shoulders.

They stayed a few more minutes, then began to yawn in an exaggerated way, and finally excused themselves, saying they were going to take a late morning nap.

Agatha turned to Tony as soon as the couple had passed out of earshot. "What was that about?"

Tony shook his head and put a finger to his lips. Agatha's eyes widened, but she held her questions.

Standing, Tony asked, "Care to walk down by the river?"

Now? She mouthed.

He nodded, so she said, "Actually I'd love that. Being stuck in an interview room all day yesterday has left me somewhat restless."

They walked side by side down the gravel path, past the cabins, to the banks of the Guadalupe. The day seemed to Tony like something from his childhood—an endless blue sky, temperatures warm enough for shorts and a t-shirt, and the water of the Guadalupe sparkling as it hurried by.

Agatha waited until they were at the banks of the river to ask in a shushed voice, "Care to share what that was about?"

Instead of answering her, he stepped closer and lowered his voice. "They were lying to us."

"You mean about the hydration pack things? But that..."

"If someone lies about the little things, they'll lie about the bigger things."

"Or perhaps he really did forget that he'd filled the hydration packs the day before."

"And perhaps Jasmine never saw Dixon on the Cox's porch."

"But why would they lie?"

"I don't know. But I plan to find out. Let's talk again about this footprint you and Gina found."

She seemed to hesitate before admitting, "It could be nothing."

"I thought so too, but this investigation has changed since we talked about it last. It's important not to discount small things or pass them off as coincidence. Sometimes the most minute details can point to something bigger."

"Like finding a single puzzle piece can open up a whole new section of the jigsaw."

"Exactly."

She recounted the events of the previous evening when she and Gina had found the footprint. Tony listened carefully and even wrote a few notes.

He was about to ask how she was holding up when the peacefulness of the morning was shattered by the sound of gunshot.

"That way," He pointed around the bend of the river. They jogged around the corner and skidded to a stop.

The Cox brothers stood knee deep in water. Both held pistols.

"What are you two doing?"

Instead of answering, they slapped at their waders and scrambled out of the water. Once they were on the bank, both dropped their guns on the ground, stripped out of their waders and continued to slap at their swimsuits.

"Problem?" Tony asked.

"Water moccasin." Mason continued to hop from foot to foot as if the snake might appear if he stood still. "I think I shot him, but there could be more."

"You shot at a snake while standing in a river? Where were you even keeping your gun?"

Instead of answering that, Paxton said, "He was coming straight at me. Man. That was a rush."

"You two aren't from around here, are you?"

Agatha had her hands on her hips and a look on her face that reminded Tony of a storm coming. He hadn't yet seen her lose her temper, but he had a feeling he was about to.

"Where are your fishing rods?" She walked

around them in a circle, as if fly rods might magically appear.

"Umm…"

"Why are you fishing here? I've told you more than once that most of my guests catch fish around the bend, in the shadows. And why are you shooting things on my property?"

Mason had the grace to look sheepish. "There was a snake, Agatha. Honest."

Agatha stomped over to Paxton, picked up his waders, shook them, and handed them back to him. "Nothing in these."

She did the same with Mason's while Tony watched on.

"Empty. Why would you think it's okay to shoot something on my property? I realize Texas is an open-carry state, but this is where I live. We have guests here."

Neither of the Cox brothers had an answer for that. They glanced at one another and seemed to silently agree that the best course of action would be to remain silent.

By the time they'd all walked back to the cabins, both men looked somewhat embarrassed, though neither had provided a reason for standing in the river with no fishing rods.

"Thanks, Agatha," Mason said.

"See you at dinner." Paxton stomped into his cabin, trailing river water.

and finally looked at him, a grave expression on her face. "I'll be careful, and I'll call you if anything else happens."

"Okay, but I have some errands to run in town. I won't be around for a few hours."

"Then I'll do my best to stay out of trouble for at least that long." With a reassuring pat on his arm, she turned and went into her house.

It was only after he was back at his own place that Tony realized he'd meant to reassure her, but in fact, she had reassured him. The problem was that he'd been here before. He'd been involved in enough murder investigations to know when danger was still afoot.

❋

Chapter Eighteen

GINA WAS still cleaning when Agatha walked back into the house. The woman never seemed to take a break. She'd apparently finished the main part of the house, scouring it from top to bottom. Now she'd turned her attention to Agatha's office. She'd been in there less than ten minutes when she called Agatha into the room.

She held up the trash can that sat under Agatha's desk and shook it. "Look at this and tell me what you think."

"Seems to be practically empty."

"Look again. Look at the wrappers."

Agatha stepped closer and peered down into the nearly empty liner. "Wrappers?"

Gina tucked the trash can in the crook of her

left arm and plucked out three wrappers. "Lemon drops. Have you started eating lemon drops?"

"*Nein.*"

"I didn't think so. In fact, I was sure you hadn't. You told me the first week I worked for you that anything lemon flavored sets your teeth on edge."

"Always has. Couldn't even eat my *mamm*'s lemon pie, which my entire family declares one of *Gotte*'s blessings."

They both stared at the wrappers in Gina's hand.

"That round Amish man eats them."

"Henry Glick?" Even as she asked, Agatha remembered he did. She'd picked up his room the day before and there had been wrappers all over the place. She'd wondered if he had a giant bag of them in his luggage.

"We both know these weren't yours, and they were right here at your desk. Henry was here."

"Oh, I'm sure there's a logical explanation."

"I checked your browser history."

"My what?"

"On your computer. Look." Gina pushed the trash can back under the desk and motioned for Agatha to sit.

Agatha had learned during Gina's first week of working for her that when the woman spoke in a certain tone it was best not to argue with her. Gina sometimes reminded Agatha of a grumpy teacher she'd had when she was in grade eight—the last grade for Amish students. She thought the woman didn't care for them at all, but then she'd caught her crying at their graduation ceremony. Apparently she had a tender heart that she kept well hidden, and Agatha expected the same was true of Gina.

She sat and stared at the laptop, though she wasn't sure what she was looking at. Computers weren't common in Amish households. In fact, they were forbidden by their *Ordnung*. Jonas had explained to her that their community allowed them for business, so she was able to have one in the office. It was battery operated, and she charged it occasionally by plugging it into the generator in the barn. She connected to the internet through a Wi-Fi hotspot which was also located in the barn.

Agatha realized many *Englischers* wouldn't understand this distinction. The truth was that Amish communities tried to limit worldly influence on their families and homes. They attempted to remain simple. It was never an easy task, and sometimes they found themselves walking a fine line between remaining plain and running a successful business.

The small laptop stayed in her office at all times. She only used it for reservations and occasionally to check the weather. Gina was already operating the mouse, clicking and moving the device left and right. Finally, she found what she was looking for.

Hands on her hips, she nodded toward the

Agatha forced her attention back to the screen, but it hadn't changed. She could only stare...stare and wonder why she was looking at a picture of Russell Dixon.

Chapter Nineteen

ᴀGATHA FOUND Henry and Jan Glick sitting and staring at the partially-demolished tennis courts.

"There's a better view down by the river."

They looked up at her. Jan attempted a smile but it slipped away, replaced by a look of pure concern. Henry waited, apparently ready for the confrontation that lay ahead.

She'd been prepared to quiz them about the web page, but looking at the couple—they weren't quite elderly, probably only five years older than she was—all her accusations fell away. Instead, she felt a deep sympathy for them, along with an intense desire to somehow make things right.

"What's wrong?" She stood in front of them,

close enough to read their expressions, but not so close as to make them feel caught. "I know it has to do with Russell Dixon. I found his...his webpage."

Henry and Jan shared a look. Jan nodded once and Henry pulled out an old pipe he carried around, though Agatha had yet to see him light it. He studied the thing as if the answers to the trials of life lay within it.

"My *dat* gave me this. He was a wise man. Had a proverb for near about everything. *Fortune favors the bold*, he'd say. By which I suppose he meant daring to change the crop in the north field, or purchasing a different type of dairy cow."

"We couldn't have known, Henry." Jan put a hand on his arm.

Henry patted her hand and raised his eyes to Agatha's. "*Dat* also said that *contentment is not getting what we want but being satisfied with what we have.*"

"That's sometimes difficult to do."

"Indeed."

"Tell me about Russell Dixon. You knew him before you came here?"

"We knew of him. He'd been to Indiana, gave a talk to prospective investors—fancy term for someone willing to plunk down their hard-earned cash."

"It was a scam?"

"Apparently."

"So you came here to confront him?"

"*Nein.*" Jan took up the story. "We simply wanted to meet with him and clarify where exactly our investment went. It's been over a year, and he promised updates but they never came."

"How much did you invest?"

"More than we should have." Henry stared out across the courts. "More than we should have."

Jan let out a long exhale. "It was our nest egg. You know how the price of land has risen in Indiana. We were hoping if we could find a way to double our money that we could help the *grandkinner* as they try to buy farmland. Now, well now it seems as if we've lost it all."

"Dixon agreed to meet with you?"

"Reluctantly." Henry ran his thumb over the bowl of the pipe, then slipped it back into his pocket. "He told us he had other business here, and that if we could make it he'd be happy to sit down with us and explain in detail where our money was and what kind of return we were receiving."

"Did the Fishers and Beilers invest as well?"

"*Ya.*"

"We'll need to all meet with Tony and possibly Lieutenant Bannister."

"The Fishers are gone."

"Gone?"

"They went back this morning."

"But they already paid for two more nights. Do you mean they went back to Indiana?"

expression grew more serious and grim with each detail. When she'd finished, he put both hands on the porch railing and looked out over his farm. It wasn't on the river, like hers, but it was good land. He'd said on several occasions how happy he was with the area, with the move they'd made.

"Do you think this is related to Mr. Dixon's death?"

"It could be." Jonas squinted his eyes, still studying the horizon. "People will kill for money. For some, money is the only achievement they have in this life. But that's not true of our people. We live this life to reflect the next, and my guess is that the Beilers and Glicks and Fishers have done a *gut* job of that. Their mistake was in forgetting our goal to remain separate—and it was a costly one, for sure and certain."

"What can we do?"

"I'll go see the two couples who are still here—counsel and pray with them. Let them know they're not the first who have fallen for a scam." He smiled for the first time since she'd delivered the news. "Remember when everyone was buying ostriches? The next great thing was going to be the ostrich burger."

"I always thought the meat had a gamey taste to it."

"But many wanted to believe they were the next great thing. Sometimes we have to be reminded

158

that the next great thing comes after this life. Our job in this one is to be good stewards with what we have."

Agatha thought of that as she turned Doc back toward the main road. *Our job is to be good stewards with what we have.* What she had was a bed and breakfast, and she planned to be the very best steward of it she could be. Even if it meant finding and confronting a killer.

Chapter Twenty

Tony's first stop was at the public defender's office. Hunt County had a single public defender, and Isabella Garcia had more cases than one person could possibly handle. He'd called ahead, and though she obviously had a full day, she'd told him to stop by.

He wasn't too surprised to see a full waiting room. The age of her clients ranged from a young woman who looked to be seventeen to an older gentleman who had to be in his seventies. Every ethnicity he could think of was represented. What they had in common was lack of resources and the need for an advocate in regard to the legal system.

A new secretary told him to take a seat, but Isabella waved Tony back into her office before he could pick up one of the dated magazines from the table.

Isabella was wearing what amounted to her work uniform—a flowered print skirt and a white blouse. Her black hair reached past her waist, and she wore it straight down her back. She was in her early thirties with dark brown skin, stood only five and a half feet, and was as round as she was tall.

As usual, her desk was perfectly clean except for a single folder. Isabella was well known for being compulsively organized. It was probably the only way she'd survived five years in the public defender's office.

"Long time, Tony."

"Been holed up in my house."

"I called a few times after the funeral—wasn't sure if you received my messages."

"I did, and I appreciate your reaching out. I suppose I've been nursing my wounds since Camilla died." Tony always found Isabella an easy person to be honest with. They'd once worked fairly closely together, and he respected both her attitude and work ethic.

"La familia, lo es todo, mi amigo."

"She certainly was everything to me."

"And grief is different for every person." Isabella centered the file folder in the middle of her desk, looked up at him, and smiled.

A kindness wafted off her that Tony had

appreciated from the first day. They were lucky to have her standing up for the rights of those who couldn't afford lawyers.

"I suppose you're here to talk to me about Russell Dixon."

"I'm impressed."

"Fairly simple deduction. Didn't take a detective to figure that out." She'd always loved teasing him about being the clever one. "First murder in our town this year."

"And hopefully, the last."

"Everyone's talking about it, and if what I read is true it happened next door to you."

"Did you know him?"

"I never met the man, but I did advise Agatha Lapp." She opened the folder, turned over the first sheet in the folder, read the second, and then glanced up at him. "She could have won a civil suit."

"Why do you say that?"

"Because insurance companies don't like facing me." Again the smile. "The driver, Willow Davis, was twenty-four years old, from Houston, and she tested clean for substances. The road was wet. The accident occurred at the curve headed out of town toward Ingram, and she was travelling at or below the speed limit."

"Apparently Dixon found that Samuel had no caution triangles on his buggy."

"True. All things combined, it was a terrible

accident and nothing more."

"So why do you say Agatha would have been awarded money from the insurance company?"

"Because they have deep pockets, and they dislike bad publicity. They would have settled out of court."

"But..."

"Your neighbor chose not to pursue civil litigation or even mediation."

Tony nodded. Agatha had told him as much.

Isabella waited the space of a heartbeat. "Can you explain that to me?"

"They're Amish. They're different."

"I gathered as much." Isabella leaned toward the sheet of paper, tilted her head, and then glanced up at him. "I remember now the thing about this case that bothered me. The insurance company didn't pay Dixon."

"So who did?"

"I never found out. I would have, but Ms. Lapp's lack of interest combined with an overly full workload..." She spread her hands out, palms up. "I had more pressing matters and there seemed no reason to look further."

"Is the fact that the insurance company didn't hire Dixon unusual?"

"It happens sometimes. I did a little digging before Agatha informed me she wasn't interested in pursuing the matter. Willow Davis didn't pay him."

"Who else would be interested in the outcome of the case?"

"A good question." Isabella closed the folder and centered it again on her desk. "Did she kill him?"

"Agatha? Kill Dixon? Not a chance."

"Then who did?"

"I have no idea."

"You're the detective."

"I was a detective."

Isabella tapped her desktop with a bright pink nail. "Once a detective, always a detective."

"I've heard that about public defenders too." Tony hesitated, then asked, "Why were you involved with this case? It's not as if Agatha had been accused of a crime. I thought public defenders represented accused persons who can't afford an attorney."

"You got me." She grinned sheepishly. "Agatha's case did not fall under my job description, but I wanted to reach out to the Amish folks here so I looked into it on my own."

"Because you have an abundance of free time."

"My thoughts were that the Amish were new to the area, probably not familiar with what can and can't happen in a court of law, and, well...the accident caught my attention."

"You're a good person, Isabella."

She stood and walked around the desk. "I've missed you. It's good to see you...out again."

"It's good to be out again."

He left her office having learned nothing but having added several additional questions to his list. Who had hired Russell Dixon? Did the same person want him dead? And how did any of this involve Agatha?

His second stop was at his insurance agent's office. David was out, but his office manager Ada was happy to talk to him. "Many policies carry an accidental death benefit now...though it is optional. Bodily injury liability is required and the minimum in Texas is thirty thousand."

"Isabella Garcia seems to think Agatha would have won a civil suit. She thinks it would've been settled in mediation."

"Most of the time that's the case. It's not worth going to court, and the insurance companies have the money. Why not just settle?"

"Doesn't that make them an easy target?"

"You can't really scam a death. You might be able to milk money for a disability or injury, but death? Sort of final. Can't spend it, either, if you're six feet under the ground."

Tony wasn't sure if he agreed with that or not. On one level, he did, but on another level what she said only added more questions. "So the woman—Willow Davis—was not at fault."

"I read the same thing in the paper."

"The insurance company knew they'd most

likely pony up thirty thousand."

"They certainly wouldn't have been surprised if it turned out that way."

"But in the end, a third party hired Dixon to throw a monkey wrench in the case. Who would do that?"

"Who would benefit from it?"

"I have no idea, but it's possible the same person might have later decided they'd benefit from Dixon's death. There are three main questions I'm concerned with now. Who is this person? Are they a threat to anyone else? Or is something or someone else standing in their way?"

He drove back toward his place, mulling over the conversation with Ada as well as Isabella. While he hadn't gleaned much new information, the bigger picture was starting to come together. He was thinking of that—of looking at things from a wider perspective—when he glanced up and noticed a black SUV in his rearview mirror. By the time he realized they meant to hit him, there was little he could do other than aim for the side of the road. They whipped past him going at least ninety.

They were barely out of sight when he received a text. Both the name and number of the caller had been blocked.

Next time we won't miss

He pocketed the cell phone, made a U-turn, and headed back to town.

Twenty minutes later, Bannister studied him across the desk.

After Tony recounted the entire incident, Bannister leaned back in his chair, hands interlaced behind his head. "You know how it is around here in the summer—teenagers acting stupid isn't exactly unusual."

"These were not teenagers."

"You were able to see them?"

"No. The window tint was too dark."

"License plates?"

"Not on the front. I didn't get a good look at the back. I was busy trying not to hit Dan Hutchison's fence."

"I don't know, Tony. I can't see that this is related to Dixon's murder."

Tony pulled out his phone, pulled up the text, and passed it to Bannister.

"Again, this could be kids messing with you. Anyone can block their number when sending a text." Bannister leaned forward, elbows braced on his desk. He looked different than he had when he'd picked up Agatha for questioning. Less cocky, a little unsure of himself, tired. Tony remembered that phase of an investigation all too well.

"I want to solve this as much as you do—more, since it's my job to catch whoever did this. But so far our best suspect is still Agatha Lapp."

"You checked out all her guests?"

He nodded once, curtly.

"No one had a connection to Dixon?"

Bannister blew out a long sigh, stood, and shut his office door. "This doesn't leave here."

"Understood."

"Dixon turned out to be a complicated fellow. We found evidence that he was running a few scams."

"What kind of scams?"

"The usual—luring in investors, promising the moon, then disappearing. Several of the couples at Agatha's place were involved."

"So you do have other suspects."

"Oh, we have a lot of those—close to a hundred, in fact. We're tracking them down, but at this point none of them were in the area at the time...other than the couples staying at Agatha's."

"What about the people at Agatha's then? Are you bringing them in for questioning?" Tony was thinking of the Cox brothers and possibly even Stuart and Brooklyn Willis.

"The guests I'm referring to were Amish. We've had them under surveillance, but if they were involved they're playing it very cool. One couple went back to Indiana, and we have their local law enforcement keeping an eye on them. So far, they haven't left the farm. Have you seen how old these people are? I don't figure them for murderers."

"Old people can murder someone."

"Sure—technically that's true, but you and I both know it doesn't usually happen."

Bannister was right. The average age of a homicide offender was late twenties to thirties. Few elderly committed such crimes.

"So why are you looking at Agatha?"

"Because she isn't as old as the others—"

"By a few years."

"She had a prior connection with the deceased—"

"As did all the people who were scammed by him."

"And she had means. Who else had a key to the cabin? Someone went in and stole his EpiPen, not to mention his phone and laptop. Plus she had a kitchen where she could bake peanut-laced muffins."

Tony waved away that point. "Anyone could have purchased those muffins in town."

"Dixon's past is unexpected. I'll admit that. I don't need to tell you we don't have the resources to track down every chump that ponied up his savings in a get-rich scheme."

"It could have been anyone, Jimmy."

"True." Jimmy Bannister studied him a moment, then recounted his case on his fingers. "But only Agatha had opportunity, means, and motive. The others lost money, but Agatha lost two members of her family."

"She didn't do it. She's Amish. Like all Amish,

she's taken a vow of nonviolence."

"A vow is one thing. Responding to tragedy is another." Bannister put his hands against his lower back. When it had made a satisfying pop, he turned his attention back to Tony. "The Amish hadn't moved here yet when you retired."

"There was talk that they would, but no one had purchased land at that point."

"They were a novelty at first, but after a few months the new wore off for some people. I'm not saying everyone. But some folks resent their kind being here."

"Their kind?"

"They work for low wages, taking jobs away from folks who grew up in this area."

"Since when is it a crime to be willing to work hard?"

"And those buggies are a problem. You know they are."

Tony wanted to argue that they were no worse than a tractor travelling down the road at twenty miles an hour, but he knew Bannister was right. The buggies took some getting used to.

"There have been some...altercations, harassment, whatever you want to call it. Now before you start in on me, we responded appropriately, but there's not much you can do when the person being harassed refuses to file a complaint. But I'll tell you, Tony..." He picked up a cold cup of coffee, drank whatever remained in it, and grimaced. "I've been there when some of those altercations took place. The Amish—the people you claim are so passive—they didn't respond in kind, but I could see a cold anger brewing. No one likes to be treated unfairly, and in my opinion, it's only a matter of time before someone snaps—vow or no vow."

"You think Agatha snapped?"

"I think anyone can be provoked to violence."

"You're wrong." Tony stood and glanced around the office one last time. He didn't miss it, not really. "You need to keep looking. Agatha did not kill Russell Dixon, and someone doesn't want me finding out who did."

On his way home, he thought about what Bannister had said. *Only Agatha had opportunity, means, and motive.* But how did they know that was true? Anyone could have snuck on the property. They could have come through the front, down the river, across Tony's place or across Daryl McNair's place.

Maybe it was time he paid Agatha's other neighbor a visit.

✳

Chapter Twenty-one

INSTEAD OF going straight home from the bishop's, Agatha drove to her friend Rebecca's farm. The Miller clan was large, owing to the fact that Rebecca, Saul and all eight of their grown children had opted to move to Texas. Rebecca's place was always full of grandchildren, and visiting her sometimes helped Agatha when she was feeling out of sorts.

She directed the buggy mare to turn into the lane and wasn't a bit surprised when Doc picked up her gait. Even the horse enjoyed visiting the Millers. Bicycles were scattered here and there across the front yard, and the garden was a riot of color. Becca was at the door before Agatha could even knock.

"I came by your place earlier in the week." Becca enfolded her in a hug then held her at arm's length. "Are you okay?"

"*Ya.* Of course. I'm fine."

Becca was the same age as Agatha—in fact, they shared a birthday month. Two inches taller and twenty pounds lighter, she felt as much like a sister as a best friend. Her blonde hair was now white, which always surprised Agatha until she remembered that her own hair had turned decidedly gray in the last year. Well, that was the way of things.

"You were at the police station."

"I can assure you that was quite an experience."

They had walked into the kitchen, where there were always a pot of coffee on the stove and fresh baked goods on the counter. These days, there was also always a baby in the playpen set up in the corner.

"Give me that *boppli*, please. I believe holding a child just might be the medicine I need today."

"Luke certainly enjoys being held. With all of his *bruders* and *schweschdern*, he spends next to no time in his crib."

Agatha stared down at the two-month-old in her arms. He'd stopped fussing and watched her as if she was the most surprising thing he'd seen all day. She found herself making cooing sounds to him, which caused him to smile, laugh, and kick out his feet.

"Oh, he's a charmer."

"For sure and certain. Put him on your

173

shoulder. He'll be out in five minutes."

By the time Agatha had recounted her visit to the Hunt Police Department, Luke was sound asleep. Becca carried him over to the playpen, then poured two cups of coffee and pushed one into Agatha's hands. "Unless you'd rather have iced tea."

"I may live in Texas, but I am still Amish."

She realized she'd missed lunch, so it didn't seem out of order to eat a few of Becca's molasses cookies. It was important that she keep up her strength. She caught Becca up on all that had occurred, sparing no details. It helped to go over everything again, to realize all that had happened in the last week.

They'd finished their coffee, and Becca had brought out her knitting. "Help me wind this yarn?"

"Of course."

She slipped her hands through the yarn and held it twelve inches apart. Doing something so simple and natural as unlooping the skein of pastel blue yarn pulled all the tension from Agatha's body.

"I needed this."

"Did you, now?"

"A little normalcy."

Two *grandkinner* ran through the kitchen, and Becca reminded them not to wake the baby.

"It's *gut* that you have so much time with your *grandkinners*."

"Do you still plan to go home in August?"

"*Ya.* It's my slowest month, and I'm looking forward to the trip."

"Having second thoughts about living so far away from your family?"

"Not at all. In fact, Marcus wrote me about coming down to stay with me next year. He's my oldest grandson and has always been the restless sort. His parents agree that time away might be good for him."

"I'm sure you'll find plenty for him to do."

"Provided I'm not in jail."

Becca paused in winding the yarn. "Tell me you're not worried that might happen."

"I know I didn't kill him, but convincing Lieutenant Bannister of that is another matter. He seems rather focused on proving it's me."

"It's a *gut* thing you have Tony on your side. He's been a real Godsend."

"And to think I barely knew him a week ago."

"Life is full of surprises. What's he like?"

"Quiet, kind, and still grieving. Though I'm not sure he realizes it. When I handed him a basket full of dinner the other night, he looked for all the world like a child who had lost his puppy. I could tell he was thinking of Camilla."

"He needs a friend, and you need a detective." Becca winked at her. "Sounds like a match made in heaven."

"I hope you're not suggesting there's anything

romantic between us."

"*Nein*." Becca pressed her lips together, but her grin widened.

"The last time you set me up with someone was a disaster."

"How was I to know Nathan loved goats so?"

"He talked about them nonstop for three hours."

"Perhaps he was nervous."

Agatha rubbed her nose with her shoulder, then motioned for Becca to continue winding the yarn. "The only way to clear my name is to find out who did this, but I can't imagine who that might be. Honestly, it's difficult for me to conceive why one person would find it necessary to kill another. I can't imagine harboring that kind of hatred."

Becca wrinkled her nose.

"What?"

"There's nothing simple about people. It seems to me that our emotions and minds don't always work together."

"Like when my mind tells me there's nothing to worry about, that *Gotte* has my life in His hands, but my heart is still beating quickly from fear."

"Exactly." Becca hesitated before going on, as if she were weighing her words. Finally she glanced up from the yarn. "Did I ever tell you about the time my *mamm* fell for a scam?"

"Your *mamm*? She was the most practical

person I've ever met, and that's saying a lot given the general no-nonsense attitude of Amish folk."

"Right? Well, this must have been...oh, twenty years ago. She was in her seventies."

"Not that old."

"Ha, ha. Remember when we were *youngies,* and we thought thirty was old?"

"Now seventy sounds like a spring chicken. Perhaps that's a lie we tell ourselves."

"Or perhaps we have a better perspective on what aging does and doesn't mean as we get older ourselves. Anyway, someone had contacted *mamm* through the phone shack. He claimed he was with the IRS and that she owed money."

They finished rolling the yarn into a ball. Becca dropped it into her knitting basket, then walked to the sink and fetched a glass of water. "It seems so long ago, but now with all this talk about Russell Dixon and his scams, well...it brings back what *mamm* went through."

"Your *dat* was already passed?"

"*Ya,* and *mamm* was living with us. Probably that's what saved her. This man told her to meet him at the bank and withdraw the money. If she did so, there wouldn't be any additional penalties." Becca pursed her lips, met Agatha's gaze, and continued. "I happened to be gathering eggs and found her hitching our old mare to the buggy. She was so agitated. I can remember it as if it were yesterday."

"So you stopped her?"

"We did, but it wasn't easy. She was absolutely certain that this person was telling the truth and that she needed to go to town and pay him. Then later, after we'd finally convinced her otherwise, she was embarrassed and also quite angry."

"He'd made a fool of her, but she had to know that wasn't her fault. That's what scammers do. They prey on people's fears and emotions."

"Exactly. Still, it took some time before she let that incident go." Becca sat back down next to Agatha, close enough that their knees were touching. "I'd find her beating rugs clean, and I'd know by the way she was taking after that dirt—she was thinking of him."

"Big difference between being angry enough to take your frustrations out on a rug and being angry enough to kill someone."

"True, but then *mamm* didn't have that much money to lose—though it was her little nest egg. Also, she had us to take care of her. Imagine if you'd lost your entire life savings."

"So you think it could have been one of the Amish couples who killed Dixon?"

"I don't know. I haven't met any of the parties involved."

"Joseph and Miriam Beiler, Jan and Henry Glick, and Ella and James Fisher. All pleasant, quiet couples, and they all seemed nice enough to me."

"But people only present the side they want us to see. That's true of Amish and *Englisch*."

Agatha felt a tightening in her chest. She took a couple of deep breaths, trying to still her heart, which suddenly acted as if she'd been the one standing outside beating rugs. "How do I know if someone is showing their true self or not?"

Becca covered Agatha's hand with her own, and that simple touch managed to calm the fear that had momentarily threatened to overwhelm her. "We will pray that *Gotte* directs your path and gives you wisdom."

"Yes, and if He could do both quickly that would be very much appreciated."

✳

Chapter Twenty-two

Tony didn't expect Daryl McNair to be home on a Friday afternoon in the middle of June, but it never hurt to try. He'd learned long ago that a good portion of being a successful detective was simply chasing down leads, no matter how obscure.

Eventually, a hunch would pay off.

Eventually, the pieces would click together.

Until then, he'd follow each and every lead.

The entrance to McNair's property was blocked by a large, ornate gate. Tony pulled up to the voice box, pushed the button, and gave his name.

"Drive through."

The gate opened and Tony pulled into an inner courtyard and parked under a portico that stretched twenty feet high and was long and wide enough for at least four large pickup trucks.

His knock was answered by a burly man in tan cargo pants and a black t-shirt stretched tightly across his chest. Apparently, the guy spent a good part of his days pumping iron at a gym. His pectoral, deltoid, and bicep muscles looked grossly inflated.

Was he even able to lower his arms down to his side?

Did he like having a neck as thick as his head?

And what was the point?

Tony was ushered into the main room with the assurance that McNair would be with him soon. The room was what some would call a great room. The ceiling rose two stories, and windows covered the east wall from the floor to the ceiling. The view of the Guadalupe River was tremendous—sunlight dancing off blue water, all beneath a cloudless sky.

The decor was a tasteful blend of modern and woodsy. Pinewood accents adorned the fireplace, bookcases, and furniture. But the nod to a country look wouldn't fool anyone. McNair had money and wasn't afraid to spend it.

Tony walked around the room, trying to get a bead on Daryl McNair. He'd met the man once or twice—they were neighbors and Hunt was a small town. But Tony didn't know much about him.

He counted at least half a dozen western sculptures, all originals by Richard Loffler according to the plaques inconspicuously placed on or near each item. Tony knew a small Loffler sculpture went for around five thousand. The ones in McNair's main room were large and detailed—probably running closer to ten thousand dollars each.

He wasn't as familiar with paintings, but a quick peek at the landscape above the fireplace mantel revealed it was a Tom Browning. He'd read in the paper that Browning's latest went for over thirty thousand dollars. McNair obviously had money, and he apparently enjoyed spending and displaying it.

Before he could snoop any further, boots echoed in the front hall and the man himself appeared in the doorway. McNair was over six feet with a military physique and buzz haircut. Though his hair had grayed at the temples, nothing else belied the man's age, which Tony thought to be in the mid-fifties.

"Detective Vargas." He crossed the room and pumped his hand.

"Actually it's just Tony—Tony Vargas."

When McNair raised an eyebrow, Tony explained, "I retired several years ago."

McNair snapped his fingers. "That's right. Your wife had a terrible illness. I read about that in the paper. My condolences." He waited until Tony acknowledged the sentiment, then released his hand and headed toward a liquor cart. Holding up a bottle, he said, "Glenfiddich, 1942. Join me?"

"Sure. Why not."

McNair didn't bother asking if he wanted it over ice. Pouring two fingers into each glass, he passed one to Tony and indicated the sitting area. "To what do I owe this visit?"

"I suppose you've heard about the murder that occurred next door—on Agatha Lapp's property."

McNair swirled the amber liquid in his glass. "I did. Of course, I did. The police came by here the same day to ask if we'd seen anything."

Tony waited.

Waiting was one of the most effective tools of any investigator.

"But I'm curious as to why you're here, since— as you say—you're no longer a detective."

"Agatha's a friend of mine."

"I see." McNair sipped the whiskey, then placed it on a marble coaster, sat back, and crossed his right foot over his left knee. "I'd be happy to help in any way I can, but I'm afraid I wasn't home that night. I had business in San Antonio, so I stayed at my penthouse."

"Was anyone here on the property?"

"I have a security team."

"And did they report seeing anything at all?"

McNair picked up his glass, stood, and walked to the windows. When he didn't return to the subject at hand, Tony joined him. He had a feeling that was what McNair expected him to do, and he was willing to play along.

"Agatha's *guests* seem to have a problem understanding property lines." He said the word *guests* as if it were the equivalent of vermin. "We've posted signs, of course, but it rarely does any good."

Tony stepped closer to the window, glanced down and saw the Cox brothers standing near the far bank—directly across from McNair's house. They were bent over and staring at something in the water, but Tony couldn't see what.

"Of course, the river is the property of the State of Texas, and I—like all the good citizens of Hunt—appreciate the tourist dollars that it brings to our good county. The problem is when they cross over to my property and tramp around, which those two have done several times." He downed the rest of the liquid in his glass. "I'm afraid no one on my staff saw a thing the night in question. They were attending a seminar over in Fredericksburg. I sent the information confirming their whereabouts to Lieutenant Bannister."

"No one is accusing your staff—"

"I understand that Bannister is just doing his job." He turned and faced Tony, smiling broadly as if the entire thing amused him. "And we wouldn't want a murderer walking around our little hamlet."

Hamlet? Seriously?

"Now. I believe this is your first visit to my home. How about I give you a tour of the place?"

"Perhaps another time."

"Certainly."

McNair walked him to the door, the epitome of a gracious host. Tony didn't mind admitting to himself that he didn't like the guy. He was wealthy, arrogant, and obviously thought he was better than everyone else. But that didn't make him a murderer. If he'd had anything to hide, it was doubtful that he'd offer a tour of the place. Besides, Tony was sure Bannister had checked out his alibi, as well as the alibi of his men.

As he walked to his truck, Tony saw the guy who'd answered the door climb into a Harley Davidson Ford F-150. With 22-inch wheels and an extended cab, Tony guessed the vehicle went for over a hundred thousand.

Every murderer had a motive. In Tony's experience, it usually boiled down to love, revenge or money.

He couldn't imagine two more different people than Russell Dixon and Daryl McNair. In fact, he couldn't think of one reason a shyster like Dixon might keep company with a millionaire like McNair—so it was difficult to imagine a motive.

Love didn't fit.

Revenge would have required their paths to cross at some point. As far as Tony could ascertain, the two men inhabited completely different worlds.

Which left money, and as he'd just witnessed, McNair seemed to have plenty.

Chapter Twenty-three

AGATHA HAD left a note on Tony's door inviting him to dinner. She'd pre-made and frozen casseroles for the week, but after visiting Becca's she had an overwhelming urge to cook. As she was setting a platter of fried chicken in the middle of the table, she was pleasantly surprised to hear a knock at the front door.

"I'll just get that."

She wiped her hands on a dish towel as she hurried toward the door. Why did her heart lift at the sight of Tony Vargas standing on her front porch? Perhaps it was just knowing he'd handled these situations before, and he wasn't intimidated about handling them again. Or maybe it was simply the joy of seeing a friend come to visit.

"Come in."

"Thank you for the invitation."

"Your timing is perfect. Everyone is gathered in the dining room."

"Agatha." He reached out and pulled her out of sight of the adjacent doorway. "I have an idea."

"About?"

He nodded toward the dining room. "Your guests are scheduled to leave on Sunday?"

"Yeah."

"So we have thirty-six hours."

"About that."

"And chances are that one of the people gathered at your table was involved in Dixon's death, or at least knows something about it."

"I can't imagine who…" She started to worry her thumbnail, then dropped her hand to her side. She wasn't a child who needed to chew on her nails, but oh, how she would be glad when this situation was resolved. "What's your idea?"

"Follow my lead?"

"Of course."

Her guests were assembled around the large dining room table, and Gina had stayed to help serve everyone. Usually, dinners weren't such elaborate affairs, but Agatha felt they all needed a pick-me-up, so she'd spent the last three hours frying and baking and sautéing.

Tony let out a long, low whistle when he saw

the spread on the table.

"Agatha went all out." Paxton Cox waved Tony over to an empty seat next to him.

"Fried chicken, mashed potatoes, gravy, and even homemade biscuits." Mason broke open a biscuit and breathed in the scent with an expression of pure bliss on his face. "I hope you brought your appetite."

"This looks and smells lovely, Agatha. I believe your cooking might be better than mine." Miriam Glick folded her hands in her lap.

"You know what they say...other people's food always tastes best."

"My *mamm* used to say that every time we went to my *grossdaddi*'s home for Sunday dinner." Joseph reached for his wife's hand, and they bowed their heads.

The Glicks and Agatha did the same. Agatha had been thanking *Gotte* for her food since she was a small child, and she wasn't going to stop because she had guests around her table...but neither did she want to make them feel uncomfortable. When she'd finished her own silent prayer, she glanced up and smiled at Brooklyn Willis.

Agatha wasn't too surprised the young mom's camera hung over the back of her chair. She'd even taken a picture of the table once they'd placed all the food on it. Now why would someone take pictures of food? Sometimes the things *Englischers* did were beyond Agatha.

"How's baby Hudson doing today?"

"Much better. Thank you for asking. And thank you for finding a high chair."

Agatha waved that away. Every Amish home kept a high chair and playpen tucked away in case they were needed. She did notice that the smile slipped from Brooklyn's face as soon as she looked down at her plate. Perhaps she wasn't feeling well, or maybe having a small child was simply exhausting. Agatha certainly remembered those days well enough.

Soon everyone was talking and enjoying the meal. Tony was sitting between Paxton Cox and Gina. Agatha was grateful Gina stayed to eat with them. Too often, she tried to slip off once the work was done, but something told Agatha the woman would enjoy a bit of socializing.

Several times throughout the meal, she noticed Tony listening and watching, but he didn't address the group until the dishes had been cleared and hot coffee poured. Agatha fetched the applesauce cake for dessert and served it with a side of fresh strawberries and whipping cream. Xavier Cooper groaned, but that didn't stop him from helping himself to a large piece.

"So how's the case going, Tony?" Jasmine sat back clasping her coffee mug. She'd barely picked at her food, and she passed on dessert as well.

Cooper was doing her best to act bored, and her husband barely acknowledged that he'd heard anything. Brooklyn was visibly shaking. Stuart was suddenly completely focused on baby Hudson, and the Glicks and Beilers stared at their now-empty dessert plates.

Tony finished his coffee, set the mug back on the placemat, and studied the group. "Would you like me to continue?"

"Yes, of course. We're enthralled." Jasmine rolled her eyes, as if her tone alone didn't convey her skepticism.

"All right. Agatha's Amish guests…the Glicks and Fishers and Beilers…all knew Dixon and had invested money in his scam. Yet on your witness forms, I suspect you checked that you didn't know the deceased."

"We did no such thing." Henry thumped his closed fist against the table. "We all agreed to leave that question blank. Besides, the question was vague. How can one ever be sure they actually know another person? We obviously did not know the real Mr. Dixon, so leaving the question blank seemed prudent."

"A lie of omission is a lie all the same."

"And we will be asking forgiveness from our *Gotte* for that." Joseph Beiler looked more tired than upset. "We've also already amended our statement with Lieutenant Bannister."

"Better late than never." Tony moved his attention around the table. "Brooklyn and Stuart, you claimed to see Dixon downstairs, when Hudson was awake and teething…but as far as I can tell Hudson isn't teething at all. If he is, he's the happiest baby I've ever seen going through the pain of cutting teeth."

The young couple glanced toward one another, but neither attempted to defend their statement.

"Jasmine and Xavier, we've already discussed the water bottle lie—"

"Misunderstanding." Xavier's voice was a low growl.

"But in fact, you haven't been hiking at all. I interviewed a woman yesterday who said you've rented kayaks every day and that she saw you just south of here on the river, with binoculars, watching. Do you want to share what you were looking for?"

Jasmine stood, pushing her chair back with a loud screech. "You're crazy. You're a burned-out cop who still wants to play detective."

She pointed a turquoise-painted fingernail at him. "And you don't know what you're talking about." She stormed from the room.

Xavier shrugged and followed her.

Which left the Cox brothers. When Tony turned his attention to them, both men seemed to shrink back.

"You two are not here to fish. I haven't

figured out what you're doing yet, but I do know it has nothing to do with Guadalupe bass. When someone's willing to lie about the little things, my experience has shown they're usually covering up something much bigger."

Paxton reached for the piece of cake he hadn't finished. "So what? It's our vacation. We can do whatever we want." But Agatha noticed his hand shook as he attempted to pile a piece of cake on the fork. He finally dropped it on the plate and stared at the opposite wall.

"So in answer to Jasmine's question, I believe the investigation is going well. All we have to figure out now is what each of you had to cover up, and whether doing so was worth committing murder."

Chapter Twenty-four

THE GROUP quickly dispersed as Agatha stood and began clearing off the dishes. She didn't seem as agitated as Tony was afraid she might be. Instead, he'd have to peg her emotions as resigned. But what did he know? A week ago he couldn't have picked her out from a line up.

"Sorry I ruined your dinner party." Tony took the stack of plates from her and carried them into the kitchen.

"I certainly wasn't expecting such a direct confrontation."

"It's about time if you ask me." Gina was already filling the sink with scalding water and detergent. She'd donned yellow rubber gloves that reached to her elbows, and when she turned to

Under different circumstances, it would have been a very pleasant vacation."

"*Danki.*"

"I believe next time I'll stick to fishing." Henry pantomimed throwing a line into the water. "This little area could become as popular as Sarasota if you don't watch out. You could be overrun with Amish."

"I wouldn't mind that one bit."

Tony sat back and listened to the banter. His Spidey-sense was telling him Henry and Joseph had more reasons for stopping by than to thank Agatha.

Joseph slipped his thumbs under his suspenders. "We thought perhaps we should start at the beginning, give you a little background on Dixon, in the hopes it will help you to solve this thing."

Pulling his pad of paper and pen from his pocket, Tony motioned for them to continue. In the fading light of a June sunset, he wrote down the salient points.

Dixon had put an advertisement in the Shipshewana paper.

He held a meeting at the local diner, in a back room.

There he showed them graphs and a flashy presentation.

It was a once-in-a-lifetime opportunity.

Half a dozen families bought in, but a year later, they'd still heard nothing regarding their investment. Finally, Henry Glick, Joseph Beiler, and James Fisher tracked the man down and insisted on a meeting. Dixon admitted he'd be at Agatha's place the following week.

"I wondered why so many reservations came in all at once, and a week before." Agatha's stared out at the Texas sunset. Finally she turned her attention back to the situation at hand. "I was happy to have a full inn—happy but surprised. Most people plan vacations further out than that."

"Wait a minute." Tony turned toward her. "How many of the people here reserved at the last minute?"

"My Amish guests and the Coopers and Mr. Dixon. Why? Is that important?"

"It might be." Tony motioned for the two men across from him to continue.

Henry nodded occasionally to confirm a point that Joseph made, but he didn't interrupt.

"Seemed like *Gotte*'s hand, *ya*?" Joseph pulled at the collar of his shirt. "An Amish Bed-and-Breakfast in the middle of Texas, where Dixon already planned to be?"

Tony wasn't ready to assign that coincidence to providence. More likely, it had been part of Dixon's plan. But the man couldn't have suspected what a deadly turn the week would take or he would have implemented more precautions. So what had gone wrong?

Henry finally jumped into the conversation. "We tried to talk to him when we first arrived. He brushed us off. Then early Wednesday morning—well before sunrise, I heard him arguing with the Cox brothers."

Tony exchanged a look with Agatha. He'd doubted Jasmine's story about Dixon's confrontation with Mason and Paxton, but apparently she'd been telling the truth.

"Any idea what the argument was about?" Agatha asked.

"Not really. I was out walking along the river because, well, I guess because I was used to rising at that hour. I heard Dixon say they should mind their own business or there would be trouble."

"Do you think Paxton and Mason had invested in Dixon's scam?"

James looked to Henry and both men shook their heads.

"Not likely," Henry said. "I don't think those Cox boys have two nickels to rub together. The truck they're driving looks worse than my last buggy, which I had for twenty years. *Nein.* I'm not sure why—or how—they happen to be here, but I don't see how they could have been investors."

Their story told, they both stood.

"Again, we'd like to offer our apologies for our dishonesty early, and we certainly never meant to be rude in any way." Joseph stood straighter—

shoulders back and head higher—as if he'd set down a heavy burden.

"Neither of you showed any rudeness to me." Agatha's words were soft and without accusation. It was obvious to Tony that their confessions only increased her sympathy for the two men.

Tony tucked his notepad and pen back into his pocket. "And if you were rude to me, I probably deserved it. Unfortunately, asking unwelcome questions is part of an investigation."

"You were only doing your job." Henry crossed his arms. "We should not have made that harder."

"Actually, I wasn't. As Jasmine pointed out, I'm no longer a detective."

Henry paused a moment, considered that, and then a smile played across his lips. "Yet a job is so much more than what you're paid to do at any given time. My job, since I was a *youngie*, has been to farm and to provide for my family. It still is my job, though these old hands no longer work a plow, and though I've lost much of what I'd saved for my family due to foolishness."

He stuffed his hands into his pockets. "That is something I will wrestle with, but I will get through it. *Gotte* doesn't lead us to trouble, but He certainly leads us through it."

"You speak the truth, Henry." Agatha rocked in her chair, her head bobbing up and down. "I've always been a homemaker. Whether it's for my family or for strangers makes little difference."

"And you, Mr. Vargas. Your job is to find the truth and to bring those who have strayed to justice." Joseph reached forward and clapped Tony on the shoulder. Somehow, that simple touch seemed like a blessing. "Yours is a higher calling, and it's likely not one that you left behind the day you retired."

Tony watched the two men walk away.

He had the distinct feeling that the pieces of the puzzle were now all on the table. The problem was, he couldn't for the life of him figure out how to put them properly together.

✱

Chapter Twenty-five

AGATHA COULD tell by the pensive expression on Tony's face that he needed a few minutes. She sat and waited and prayed that God would ease this man's mind.

She'd often seen that look of consternation on her own husband's face. Seth had been a kind and gentle man. And quiet, which perhaps wasn't that unusual for a Plain person. She could always tell when he needed to think—to make connections and draw lines. They'd shared twenty-four years of marriage, and in that time she'd learned to be patient and give him that space.

When Tony finally turned to look at her the sky had darkened and the porch's solar lighting had switched on.

He smiled ruefully. "You probably wish I'd go home."

"Not at all." She hesitated, then said what had been on her mind probably since Wednesday morning. "You probably wished I'd run the opposite direction when I found Dixon's body. If I'd gone south, Mr. McNair would have caught the brunt of this mess. Or if I'd just gone inside and used the office phone to call the police..."

"I don't regret becoming involved."

"You don't?"

"As Joseph pointed out, solving who committed a crime—finding the truth—it's what I do. Besides, if it hadn't been for Dixon's murder, we might have remained polite neighbors and nothing more. Just think, I never would have sampled your cooking."

"Now that would have been a real tragedy." Agatha wanted to offer some kind of solace to the man sitting beside her, but she wasn't sure quite how. Something in Tony's voice told her he was wrestling with a great hurt and perhaps trying to cover it up with light words.

So again, she waited.

Finally, he pointed in the direction Henry and Joseph had left. "Those two men have given me a great deal to think about."

"In regard to Dixon's murder?"

"Not really." He repositioned the rocker so he was facing her more directly, studied her, and finally shook his head. "They've suffered a great loss, but they're not dwelling on it. Instead, they're doing what they can to make things right, and they're moving on."

"Their actions convey their intent to move forward, but the hurt and embarrassment will no doubt linger for some time. Don't let their common sense ways fool you. Amish men—and women—are no different from *Englisch* in many ways. Humiliation is a bitter pill to swallow."

"My point is, they're moving on." He stood and paced in front of her. When he finally turned her direction, she understood his struggle wasn't really about the murder investigation at all. "I, on the other hand, have been sitting in that house feeling sorry for myself for nearly a year."

"Losing money is not the same thing as losing a person."

"Camilla would give me a good swift kick in the backside if she could. She told me, just before she died, she said, 'Don't waste your life, Tony. It's a gift. Live it.'"

"She sounds like a special person. Did you have any children?"

"No. She couldn't, and it never mattered. It was enough that we had each other."

She thought he might leave then. Instead, he rested his backside against the porch railing. "You're a widow."

"I am."

"Children?"

"Four sons and a daughter—all grown with families of their own." Fonzi made an appearance, meowing and winding between Agatha's legs. She reached down and stroked the cat, causing it to purr like a small engine.

"Was it hard to leave them?"

"To come here? Yes and no. I knew they would visit, and I needed...I suppose I needed a purpose. Or maybe I was just looking for an adventure."

"How did you...handle it?"

"It?"

"Being a widow—the loneliness, the grief. Even regret, maybe."

Agatha didn't answer right away. She rocked a minute, closed her eyes, and allowed the breeze to calm her heart and mind. Finally she stood, walked to Tony's side, and they both turned and stared out over the porch railing at moonlight skipping off the river.

"Those things you speak of...they're a natural part of heartache. Seth, he was a *gut* husband, and I lost him too early. At the time, I couldn't even think about caring for someone else, so I threw myself into raising my children and providing a home for them. But even as I washed clothes and made meals and helped my *kinder* with their schoolwork, the shadow of my grief was there."

She turned to him and smiled, though she realized he probably couldn't see that. "I can't tell you when the first day was that I woke without that heaviness in my heart. And I can't tell you that I don't still feel it on occasion. But most days...now... are filled with fond memories of him. The ache has taken a back seat to an appreciation for the time we shared. Mainly I'm grateful for that—to have known and loved him."

"I like to think that I could take such a mature attitude someday, but I'm not sure I ever will."

"Oh, it's not about maturity, Tony. We get up every day, put on our clothes, and go about our business. I had no choice because my children depended on me."

"While I've had the luxury of wallowing in my pain."

"Perhaps *Gotte* knew you needed that time, and perhaps one man's wallowing is another man's path to healing."

Agatha followed him to the porch steps. "Will you call Bannister? Update him on what we've learned?"

"I'm not sure we've learned anything, except that everyone was hiding something. That's not unusual. People have lives—have struggles—that we can't begin to imagine."

"You still think one of my guests was involved."

"I do. The question is which one."

He said goodnight, and Agatha watched him walk across her yard to his property. He paused at his side door to wave, then disappeared into his home. Fonzi curled up in the rocker she'd just vacated, winking at her and closing his eyes.

Agatha walked around her kitchen and living area, adjusting a pillow here, wiping away a speck of dust there. In truth, there was little to do. Gina cleaned everything within an inch of its life. But Agatha was restless and not ready to turn in for the night.

What were the Cox brothers doing on the river?

Why had Jasmine and Xavier rented a kayak? Who were they spying on?

What were Brooklyn and Stuart hiding?

As for the Beilers and the Glicks and the Fishers, Agatha did not—could not—believe they were in any way involved. Not because they were Amish... even Amish sometimes succumbed to passion and bad decisions. No, it was more that they were so obviously subdued by what had happened to them. She didn't sense a terrible rage there, only a deep sadness.

She readied for sleep—combing out her hair and loosely braiding it, washing her face, brushing her teeth. The routine calmed her. Finally, she climbed into bed and opened her Bible. She read a chapter each night—something her parents had begun with her when she was a small child.

She tended to enjoy the Psalms or Proverbs before bed, sometimes Isaiah or even Job. Yes, she could certainly relate to Job's questions. But this evening she pulled her battery-operated lantern closer, fumbled with her glasses, and turned to the book of Romans. It took her a few moments to find the passage she sought, her fingers casting long shadows across the page as she traced the words.

When she found it, she released a breath she hadn't realized she was holding.

But we also rejoice in our suffering because we know that suffering produces perseverance, perseverance character, and character hope. And hope does not disappoint...

Hope does not disappoint.

The words calmed her heart and helped her slide into a dreamless, restful sleep.

Chapter Twenty-six

REAKFAST WENT well the next morning, meaning no more dead bodies popped up and everyone seemed to have recovered from Tony's grilling the night before. After they'd cleared off the dishes, Gina set off to give the cabins a brisk cleaning while Agatha headed to work in her garden.

Doc was in the pasture grazing. She paid an Amish teen to stop by early in the morning and again in the evening to care for the horse. Now the mare raised her head as if to nod at Agatha. It was such a beautiful sight—such a simple sight—just a mare in a field on a pleasant June morning. She often found that thirty minutes of pulling weeds set her day on the right track, and she'd slept so well the night before that she felt full of spunk and energy.

At least, she did until she turned the corner behind the barn. Then the energy faded out of her like water poured from a pitcher and her knees went suddenly wobbly.

Because when she turned to enter the garden area, she saw a message painted in sloppy, broad strokes on the back of her barn wall.

DEAD WRONG

That was it.

Just those two words.

What could it possibly mean? It looked as if the graffiti artist had used the left over paint from her wraparound porch. She stepped closer and placed a finger against the letter D. Definitely Swiss Coffee. She'd spent enough time staring at paint chips to recognize the color she'd picked for her front porch trim. From a distance, the message might not even be noticeable. But up close, the off-white stood out against the gray, which was called Silvery Moonlight.

She'd been so proud of her newly painted barn.

Pride goes before destruction, a haughty spirit before a fall. The Proverb popped into her mind, but she pushed it away. She didn't think pride in a cleanly-painted barn had been such a sin, and it certainly hadn't caused Russell Dixon's destruction.

Whoever painted the graffiti had apparently been in a hurry. The paint dripped toward the ground with each letter, giving it a macabre effect.

Who was dead wrong?

About what?

And who had left the message on the side of her barn?

She was trying to decide whether to go in the house and call Tony or continue with her gardening when Gina skidded around the corner of the barn. She was out of breath and flushed. She stopped with one hand on her hip and the other pressed to her chest. Her posture was slightly bent as she tried to pull in a deep breath.

"Are you all right?"

Gina held up a finger.

"Should I fetch you some water?"

"No." She glanced up at Agatha, and that was when she caught sight of the message. Her mouth fell open, but no words escaped.

"I know. They didn't even do a good job of the painting. It's a mess. Look, it dripped all down the wall."

"What does it mean?"

"I have no idea." Agatha stepped closer to her friend. "What's wrong? Why were you running?"

"It's the Cox brothers."

"What about them?"

"They're gone."

"Gone?"

"And they left a note."

Agatha hurried with Gina back to Cabin 2.

The rooms weren't exactly spotless, but they were empty. No fishing equipment. No food. No clothing.

"They're gone." Agatha turned in a circle, trying to understand what she was seeing—or rather what she wasn't seeing.

"Yeah. That's what I said." Gina stomped across the room and pointed to a single sheet of paper on the counter, held down by a pepper shaker as if the writer feared a strong wind might come through the cabin and blow the note away. "I didn't pick it up—in case they want to dust it for fingerprints."

"Why would they do that?"

"Because the Cox brothers could be the killers."

"If they were, and I'm not saying I believe that, their fingerprints are all over this room."

Gina sniffed and raised her chin a fraction of an inch. "Not if they wiped it down."

"Wiped it down? Can you hear yourself? And did you ever see Mason or Paxton wipe down anything...including their feet?"

"Valid point."

Agatha stared down at the note. Like the message on her barn wall, it only had two words, so it didn't take long to read.

We're Sorry

"Sorry for what?" Agatha asked.

"I was wondering the same thing. Did they pay their bill?"

"*Ya.* Paid in full when they first checked in. All my guests do, since they check out on Sunday and I'm at church when they leave."

"Maybe they're apologizing for killing Dixon."

"Really? You think they'd leave a note that would confess to the crime?"

"I don't know." Gina's hands fluttered in front of her like two birds suddenly gone wild. "I don't know what's going on here, but two people left you a note since Tony's interrogation session last night. I think one of them must have killed Dixon."

An hour later Agatha's place was once again overrun with Hunt County PD.

"Bannister and Tony seem like old chums," Gina noted.

"I believe they've put aside their differences to solve the case."

Bannister said something to Tony that caused him to frown, look off toward the river, and nod once. Whatever it was, the lieutenant had made a decision. He pulled out his radio and walked away as he talked into it.

Tony made his way back to Gina and Agatha. The rest of the guests had been mildly interested the first fifteen minutes, then drifted off to do other things. It seemed the murder mystery no longer held their attention, but then it was the last full day of their vacation. Perhaps they had other activities planned for the morning—activities like picnics and walks by the river and resting in a hammock.

"Bannister had turned up some information on Mason and Paxton," Tony said. "He was coming out to question them today."

"What kind of information?" Agatha felt a frown forming between her eyes and she reached up with her forefinger to rub it away. The last thing she needed was a headache from scrunching up her face.

"I'm not at liberty to go into detail, but they have some financial problems—enough to constitute motive."

"How would killing Russell Dixon net them any money?" Gina asked.

"Good question, and Bannister is working on that. But the note—that seems to indicate they did something wrong."

"Could be a confession." Gina's voice took on a decidedly cheerier tone. She threw a told-you-so look at Agatha.

"Bannister thinks it's the break we've been waiting for. If the Cox brothers—"

"Stop it, both of you." Agatha stomped her foot, then felt foolish so she offered a weak smile. "I liked those boys. I know their manners were lacking and they were a bit daft when it came to fishing, but I think they both had a good heart."

"A good heart? You're crossing two suspects off the list because you think they had a good heart?"

Gina folded her arms over her chest. "Not good enough, Agatha."

Tony was fighting a smile. Agatha had learned he had a marked frown when he was trying not to laugh. No doubt he found it quite funny that two older ladies—one Amish, one *Englisch*—might be able to solve a murder. Which wasn't a fair assessment of Tony at all. He'd been nothing but respectful and kind to her. She was simply feeling a bit off. The day was not going as she'd hoped.

"Given Jasmine's testimony that she saw them arguing with Dixon, along with their suspicious behavior this week—"

"Suspicious how?" Agatha fought to lower her voice. "Explain that to me, Tony."

"Look. I get it. They were your guests. But I'm telling you, those boys were hiding something. They definitely were not fishing in the Guadalupe all week. Add in their financial problems, the note, and their sudden disappearance, and it's enough for Bannister to release an All-Points Bulletin for their apprehension."

Agatha couldn't believe what she was hearing. She also couldn't explain why she felt suddenly defensive regarding Mason and Paxton.

"As for the paint on the barn, that seems to be nothing more than a prank. Maybe high school students did it. We might look into getting you some security cameras or outside lighting."

"No, we will not." Agatha had heard quite enough. "This is still a Plain Bed-and-Breakfast, and I will not be adding cameras to spy on my guests or bright lights which will dim the evening stars."

"She's stubborn," Gina said under her breath.

"And a bit behind the times," Tony added.

"I can hear you both." She wanted to remain aggravated, but when Gina and Tony smiled at her, she couldn't hold on to it. "What do we do now?"

"I'm headed into town. There were a couple of loose ends I wanted to follow up on, though if Bannister is right...we might be close to solving this." He reached out and gave her an awkward pat on the shoulder, causing Gina to raise an eyebrow. "I'll be in touch."

They stood there and watched him walk away.

"He'll be in touch?"

"That's what he said."

"Say, are you two—"

"Stop right there. The answer is no."

Gina might not believe her, but at least she dropped the topic. Once again, Agatha's property seemed to be returning to normal. Tony was gone, the guests had returned to their various amusements, and Bannister and his crew were packing up. Agatha was trying to decide between going back to the garden or fixing a light lunch when Gina grabbed her arm.

"Ouch."

"Sorry, but look."

"Look at what?"

"Brooklyn."

"What about her? She's taking pictures of the baby. She's always taking pictures." Agatha wondered if maybe Gina needed a vacation. Perhaps the murder and investigation had been too much for her. She'd pulled in her bottom lip and when she turned toward Agatha, her eyes were wide.

As they watched, Stuart picked up baby Hudson, and the couple walked toward their vehicle, plopped the baby into the infant seat, and started the car.

Lowering her voice, Gina said, "I cleaned their room first thing this morning."

"Okay."

"I didn't realize...I didn't put it together until just now."

Stuart started the car, and slowly and carefully pulled out onto the road.

"You didn't put what together?"

This time Gina grabbed Agatha's arm in both of her hands.

"The paint...there were drops of paint on the floor. I wondered where it came from, but I hadn't seen what was on the barn yet. It wasn't much. Only a few drops."

"But you're sure?"

"Yes. I'm sure. Either Brooklyn or Stuart left

you that message on the barn."

"All right."

"All right?"

"All right. We'll ask them what it means."

"Just like that?"

"Sure. As soon as they return."

"You mean *if* they return."

Which Agatha thought was nothing more than Gina adding one more dramatic statement on top of an already overly-dramatic situation. Though she couldn't resist the urge to stop by their suite of rooms upstairs in the main house—just to be sure their suitcases were still there.

They were, which might mean they were coming back.

Or it could mean they were more concerned about getting away than they were about their belongings.

Chapter Twenty-seven

Tony realized that what they had on the Cox brothers was flimsy at best. They could have been apologizing for anything, and a part of him sympathized with Agatha. The two seemed like puppies that had been raised with little or no training, but they didn't strike him as inherently bad or desperate.

The problem was that they were hiding something.

Everyone was hiding something, which wasn't so unusual. People rarely exposed their true selves to the world. Sometimes the reasons for keeping secrets were understandable, and Tony might even do the same in their situation. But other times, what was being hidden didn't make sense. Like a thread he'd once pulled on a sweater Camilla knit for him, tug hard enough and the entire thing came unraveled.

That's what he wanted to do for the next few hours.

He wanted to tug on a few loose threads.

Because this case was coming together. Possibly the killer was being pushed into a desperate and ill-timed move, in which case they'd catch him or her. Or maybe the time frame was simply closing. Agatha's guests would all be gone the next day. Tony knew few cases were solved in less than a week, but he felt they were very close.

His first stop was at the small fishing shop in downtown Hunt. Tony tapped around on his phone until he pulled up a picture of Paxton and Mason that Bannister had forwarded to him.

"Have you ever seen these two?"

"Sure."

Dan Littlefield had been in trouble a few times as a teenager. Tony had picked him up once himself—kid was walking down the side of the road too drunk to know he was headed out of town instead of toward it. Dan had changed since those days as a malcontent teenager. He'd found his passion in the Guadalupe River and the little shop on Main Street. Little Bait and Tackle, a play off his name, had an excellent reputation throughout the Hill Country. If you wanted to know what fish were biting and what fly or lure to use, Dan was the man to ask.

He'd turned thirty a few months before. His hair was pulled back in a ponytail, and a few tats danced down his browned arms—but his eyes were clear and his hands steady. It did Tony's heart good to see how the man had turned his life around.

"They were in here earlier in the week. Staying at Agatha's, right?"

"That's right."

"Paper says there was a murder out there earlier this week."

"We can always count on the Hunt County News to keep our citizens informed."

Dan grunted and turned off the light on the magnifying glass he'd been using. He set aside the fly he'd been tying and cracked his neck to the left and then right.

"Those two stopped by here, but they weren't interested in fishing."

"They didn't buy anything?"

"Oh, they bought a few things, but when I told them they wouldn't catch any fish with the kind of flies they were buying they only shrugged and added another package."

"Can you explain that?"

"Not really. People are strange."

"Agreed, but those two—well, in some ways they struck me as harmless."

Dan patted his pocket, then grimaced. "Giving

up smoking has been twice as hard as staying sober."

"But worth the effort."

"I guess." Dan grabbed a bottle of water and downed half of it. "My impression, which is worth less than this bottle of water, is that they wanted to look like fishermen."

"But why?"

"I have no idea. Like I said—people are strange."

"All right. Well, thanks for your help."

Tony was pushing his way back out onto the sidewalk when Dan called out to him. "I happened to be closing up just after their sale. When I walked out to my jeep, they were still parked out front, rearranging things in the back of their truck."

Tony waited, aware that the hairs on his neck were standing on end.

"Catch a glimpse of something?"

"Boots, buckets, a shovel, and pans."

"Pans?"

"Yup. They didn't look like what you'd use on the stove—more battered. Plus, I wondered why they'd need them if they were staying at Agatha's. She's one of the best cooks in the area."

"Yeah, she is. Thanks, Dan."

"Any time."

Tony's next stop was the kayak rental spot on the outskirts of town. Patti Baker was squirting off a row of kayaks lying in the sun, bottoms up.

"Patti."

"Tony. Surprised to see you here twice in two days."

"Wanted to ask you a couple more questions."

Patti was what the courts would call a hostile witness. She didn't like Tony, and she made no attempt to hide it. He'd been instrumental in busting up a drug ring five years earlier, and her son had been caught in that net. He was currently serving five to ten years in the care of the State of Texas.

"Don't suppose I can stop you from asking."

Actually, she could. She had every right to ask him to leave, but Tony didn't think pointing that out would be the best way to get his answers.

"You told me when I stopped by before that you rented a kayak to Jasmine and Xavier Cooper…"

"And later saw them sitting south of Agatha's, spying on her place with binoculars. I remember what I said."

"Anything else come to mind since I spoke with you yesterday?"

"About those two? Not a thing." She began flipping the kayaks over. Tony was tempted to offer to help, but one pointed look from Patti changed his mind.

"What about these two? Have you rented to them?"

He stepped closer and showed her pictures of the Cox brothers. Patti shook her head once—a curt, definitive motion.

"And what about these two?" This time he showed her a picture of Stuart and Brooklyn. "They would've had a baby with them."

"I don't recommend that people with small children go out on kayaks."

"So you didn't rent to them?"

"I did not."

"Haven't seen them?"

"I haven't seen any of them here at my shop. Those two men, I saw them in the river, as I was guiding my group past."

"They were fishing?"

"No. Not that I could tell."

"So what were they doing?"

"Your guess is good as mine—maybe better, what with you having been a detective and all."

Tony pushed his phone into his pocket. He hadn't learned anything, but then he hadn't really expected to. Mainly he was tugging on the case's loose ends. He was missing something, but whatever it was lurked just out of his field of vision.

"I guess you've seen the new signs." Patti's back was to him, so he had to step closer to clearly hear what she said.

"What signs?"

"On McNair's property."

"No, I haven't."

"I'm telling you. People around here need

to wake up." She squirted the row of kayaks with renewed vigor, as if they were to blame for people not being awake. "If we don't watch out, this place is going to turn into another Fredericksburg, and that isn't going to be a good thing for the town or the river. You think we had drug problems before? A place like that only brings in more trouble, more people who don't belong."

"Patti, I don't know what you're talking about."

"Put in on the far side of McNair's place and paddle toward yours. You'll see them." She shut off the water, tossed the hose to the side, and trudged off to the small hut that was her office.

She didn't offer to rent him a kayak, but then Tony didn't need one. He'd bought one years ago when he and Camilla were dreaming of their retirement. The Lifetime Sport Fisher Angler 100 had set him back six hundred dollars. He'd put it in the water twice—both times before her diagnosis. Since then it had been hanging in his garage. Sounded like it was time to pull it out.

An hour later he was on the river.

He had to put in half a mile south of McNair's, because that was the first public access. He could have put in from his own place, but then he'd have to cross Agatha's. At this point, something told him it would be best to proceed as unobtrusively as possible.

Towering pecan and cypress trees lined the

bank. The upper portion of the river ran through the towns of Kerrville, Hunt, Ingram, Comfort, and Boerne. The southern portion, which was inundated with tourists, river floaters, swimmers, and fishermen, went through New Braunfels and Gruene.

The congestion and subsequent litter became such a problem that New Braunfels passed a law banning disposable food and beverage containers on the river. Although the river itself belonged to the State of Texas and was open to all, access to the river was limited because the land that bordered it was largely privately owned.

It was a constant source of tension to find the right balance between tourist dollars, people's right to enjoy the river, and landowners' rights for privacy.

But those problems hadn't reached Hunt.

This part of the river was still serene. Unspoiled. Patti was right when she said people needed to be aware of the cost of development, and money was just the beginning of it. Many folks would fight to keep the area undeveloped. They saw it as their responsibility to protect the river.

The area across from Tony's place, Agatha's, and McNair's was owned by a youth camp. Much of it was undeveloped though most evenings the kids staying at the camp trekked down to the river and used an old rope swing to plunge into its cold water. As Tony paddled around a bend that led to McNair's property, the river widened.

It didn't take him long to find the signs Patti mentioned.

Coming soon

The Guadalupe Resort

Private Property. No Trespassing.

Tony stared at the sign for several moments.

What was The Guadalupe Resort? He hadn't heard of it. No one had mentioned it, and from what he could see with his binoculars, nothing had been done on McNair's property. Had the development been in the local news and he'd simply missed it? If Patti Baker knew about it, it must be public knowledge.

But McNair hadn't mentioned it.

He'd complained about Agatha's guests, and he'd mentioned...what was it? He said he'd posted signs about the river frontage being private property. He'd changed the subject then and offered to give Tony a tour of the place. Staring at McNair's property now through his binoculars, Tony wished he'd accepted that offer.

Sun glinted off the second story windows, but he didn't see any activity on the property at all. In fact, it seemed completely devoid of people.

Tony paddled back to his truck, loaded the kayak, and once again turned toward town.

He didn't know whether McNair's development plans had anything to do with Dixon's murder—seemed a stretch to think it would. McNair had offered an alibi for himself and his men, and Bannister had checked it out.

Correction.

McNair said Bannister checked it out. Had he?

One more question he needed answered.

But first, it was time to visit an old friend.

Chapter Twenty-eight

S TUART AND Brooklyn didn't return until well after lunch.

Gina hung around to provide moral backup, or maybe because she thought Agatha wouldn't be aggressive enough in her questioning.

"You baked them cookies? You think the way to make them confess is…" She picked one up, broke off a piece and popped it into her mouth. "Oatmeal?"

"Oatmeal raisin with nuts."

"Nuts are what got us into this trouble in the first place."

"Cooks and bakers know the secret to a good day is patience."

"Is that another one of your proverbs?"

"It is."

"Any idea what it means?"

"Stick around and you'll find out."

Stuart apparently couldn't resist the scent of freshly-baked cookies. He walked into the room, carrying a very sleepy Hudson. Brooklyn followed them into the kitchen, though she held back at the door.

Agatha poured Stuart a tall glass of cold milk and pushed the platter of still-warm cookies toward him. He practically melted into the chair. Brooklyn sighed deeply, then joined him at the table, removing her camera strap from her around her neck and placing the device on the table. She didn't sit so much as perch on the edge of her chair, as if she needed to be ready to flee.

Agatha started by asking them how their day was going. They'd taken Hudson to a local farm that had a small petting zoo.

"He especially liked the baby goats." Stuart kissed his son's hair.

"Don't we all?" Agatha said. "I've thought of getting a few to help with the lawn around here."

Hudson was fast asleep against his father. There was no doubt that both Stuart and Brooklyn dearly loved their child. There was also no doubt in Agatha's mind that they had not killed Russell Dixon, but they knew something.

Agatha turned her attention to Brooklyn,

but she apparently had nothing to add to the conversation. Dark circles rimmed her eyes, and she tapped an erratic pattern on the kitchen table with her thumb. Agatha's heart went out to the woman, but one look from Gina firmed up her resolve to find out what was going on.

"I guess you all heard about the Cox brothers leaving."

Stuart's head bobbed as he reached for another cookie. He offered one to his wife who waved it away. She still hadn't looked directly at Agatha or Gina.

"And the painting on the barn? Did you see that, too?"

Now Brooklyn's eyes widened, and she looked up before jerking her gaze away and pulling Hudson from Stuart's arms.

Apparently Agatha was taking too long to get to the point, because Gina jumped in.

"Couldn't help noticing when I cleaned your room that there were some paint spots on the floor. Paint spots the same color as the message splashed across Agatha's barn. So which one of you did it?"

So much for being subtle.

Agatha folded one hand over the other. "Not that we're accusing you of anything, but...well, can you explain that?"

Brooklyn clutched Hudson to her chest, as if Agatha might grab the child and run off with him.

Stuart sighed heavily, then put an arm across the back of his wife's chair. Leaning toward her, he said, "We need to tell them. We can trust Agatha and Gina. And we need to tell someone."

Brooklyn glanced at Stuart, and if anything she paled even more.

"Whatever it is, I assure you that you can trust us. We only want to figure out what's going on. I'm trying to run a business here, and I want this to be a restful, peaceful place, not one where my guests are plainly terrified."

Brooklyn finally raised her gaze to Agatha's, and when she did her resolve crumbled. "I didn't know what else to do. You all are on the wrong track."

"We're dead wrong?"

"Yes! But I couldn't come right out and tell you. If they know I know, if they know about the picture, we could be next. I wanted to just leave, but Stuart said—"

"I said we needed to act normal." He sat back and rubbed a hand across his face. "I don't know if we're in any real danger or not, but I felt it was better to act as if each day is just another day on vacation."

"Perhaps if we take things from the beginning," Agatha said. "But first let's get you a glass of water."

Gina jumped up to fill a glass from the pitcher in the refrigerator. By the time she'd handed it to Brooklyn, Stuart had taken the baby back into his

"Now show us what's on that camera," Gina said.

Twenty minutes later, the Willis family was upstairs taking a nap. Agatha had penned a note and stuck it on Tony's door.

"You could just text him."

"I don't have a phone that texts."

"I do."

"Well, I don't think it's that kind of emergency."

"It's something."

"Yes, it is."

"We have to get into McNair's."

"Oh, I don't know about that."

"Her picture plainly showed someone walking from McNair's to your place, at the exact moment Dixon was out of his cabin arguing with the Cox brothers."

"What could that possibly mean?"

"It means the Cox brothers were distracting him while someone else snuck onto your property and changed his food with a peanut-laced muffin—a muffin that killed him."

"I don't know. Something's missing in your assessment."

"I agree, and whatever it is, we might be able to find it in McNair's house."

Agatha turned and studied her friend, and Gina was that—her friend as much as her employee. They were standing next to Gina's car. "Even if that's true, I can't break into McNair's house. I can't do that. It's wrong. It's trespassing. It's illegal, and I won't do it."

If she'd thought that mini-lecture would temper Gina's enthusiasm, she was sorely mistaken.

"What if I can get us in there, without breaking in?"

"How would you do that?"

"Just let me handle it. You're going to be here the rest of the day?"

"*Ya*. Sure, I am."

"Then I'll be back. It could be later—after dark for sure. Wait for me, okay?"

Which seemed a silly thing to ask, because Agatha had nowhere else to go and nowhere else she wanted to be.

❋

Chapter Twenty-nine

Tony had gone to the local real estate office, but his old friend Charles wasn't in.

"Fishing—again. Says he can sell a house from his boat same as he can from his desk." The receptionist, who couldn't have been over nineteen, shrugged and resumed tapping on her cell phone.

"Did he say where he was fishing?" When she didn't answer, he leaned across the reception desk and put his hand between her phone and her eyes. She glanced up, clearly surprised he was still there.

"What?"

"Where did he go fishing?"

"North Fork of the river—I'm not really sure where."

Tony was already walking out. He knew where.

Charles had a favorite spot along the North Fork. They'd fished there together a dozen times, and it would explain why he wasn't answering his texts—cell service that direction was notoriously terrible.

The sun was inching lower by the time Tony pulled up behind Charles's crew cab truck. Five minutes later he'd snagged a cold Dr. Pepper from his friend's cooler and was watching him pull in a nice-sized bass.

"I know you didn't come out here to drink my soda and watch me fish."

Charles was Tony's age. Tony and Camilla had purchased their house through him. Charles's wife was a teacher at the Hunt middle school, and the two couples had developed a close friendship. Since Camilla's death, Tony had ignored his friend's calls and texts. He regretted that now, but it wasn't the time to explain why he'd been hiding away for ten months. He needed answers, and something told him he needed them quickly.

"Tell me about the Guadalupe Resort."

"Not much to tell, since it doesn't exist yet."

"But McNair has a plan for one?"

"He does. I haven't seen the drawings myself, but rumor is that he has investors."

"Has he presented anything to the city council?"

"He has not." Charles skillfully pulled the barbless hook from the fish's mouth, then set it gently back into the water.

"How big is it?"

"The resort? Big, if you believe the rumors."

"Do you?"

Charles stopped what he was doing and peered at him from underneath his fishing hat. "McNair's always been an ambitious fellow."

"Meaning?"

Instead of casting his hook back out into the water, Charles took a seat on the log beside Tony, pulled out a bottle of iced tea, and uncapped it. When he'd drank a third of it, he recapped it and cleared his throat.

"There's been noise about McNair's development for a little over a year. This is all scuttlebutt, mind you, but it's from people that generally know what they're talking about. He came up with this big plan to bring a five-star resort to our area, and even procured a few investors."

"I'm hearing a 'but' coming up."

"Something threw a monkey wrench into his plans."

"What?"

"I don't know. Nobody seemed to be surprised. You know how it is—there's always rumors of some big development, but then something happens and it falls apart. Anyway, when his plans fell through everyone thought it was par for the course, and we didn't give it much thought."

"I'm sensing this isn't the end of the story."

"Ten months ago, the talk starts up again. Whatever was impeding his plans suddenly wasn't, and more investors were signing on."

"And then what?"

"Nothing. That's the last I heard."

Tony told him about the signs on McNair's property.

"Anyone can make a sign. Probably had them put there for investors that came out to take a tour of the site."

"Wait a minute. What site?"

"The site for his resort. Maybe you need to slow down on that Dr. Pepper. The sugar content might be messing with your brain processing."

Tony stood up and pulled his keys out of his pocket. "The resort was going to be on McNair's property?"

"That's what I heard."

"How big was it going to be?"

"Your guess is as good as mine. Big, though, like I said. Big enough that he was flying investors in to see it. An agent I know in San Antonio asked me about it recently, and another in Houston mentioned it during a conference call."

"But he doesn't own that much land."

Charles shrugged and stuck the bottle of iced tea back in the cooler. "Guess he found a way to buy some more."

"I need to go."

"Hey. Are you okay?"

"Ask me tomorrow."

It was an hour back to Agatha's, and the sun had already sunk below the horizon. It would be fully dark well before he made it back. But as he sped toward her B&B, he realized Agatha's place wasn't where he needed to go first.

He needed to go to McNair's.

He needed to figure out what was going on, and if whatever it was had been worth killing for.

Chapter Thirty

*A*GATHA WAS turning off the last lantern and about to lock the front door when Gina appeared out of the darkness.

"You took a year off my life." Agatha pushed the screen door open. "Come inside. What are you doing out this late?"

"I got us in."

"In?"

"Next door."

"Oh."

"You know you'd like to see what's going on over there."

Agatha turned lanterns on again as they moved through the house. When they reached the kitchen, Gina began pulling items out of her shoulder bag.

"What are these?"

"They're part of our uniform."

"Our uniform?"

"There's bound to be cameras. We need to look like we belong. This is our disguise. See? It says Merry Maids across the top of the ball cap."

Agatha reached for her glasses, couldn't find them, brought the cap closer, then held it at arm's length. Either way, it was plain as day that Merry Maids had been penned on with permanent marker.

"This won't fool anyone."

"It's nine o'clock at night, and my source..."

"You have a source?"

"A guy who does security over there...Nate."

"Nate Luscombe?"

"How do you know Nate?" Gina cocked her head to the side and stared at her as if she'd sprouted bunny ears.

"He did a little work here when I first moved in...before I knew you."

"Nate's handy. And now he's doing security work next door. He said he could get us in, but we have to hurry. He makes his rounds every half hour. So we have..." She glanced at her watch. "Fifteen minutes before he leaves the front gate."

"We want him to leave?"

"No, we want him to be there so he can let us in. Now go put on your blue jeans and this t-shirt." The t-shirt had also been haphazardly decorated with the words Merry Maids, and to add more credibility a broom and dustpan as well. "I know you have blue jeans. You wore them that time we cleaned out the back room of the barn."

"*Ya*, but I only wear them in an emergency."

"This is an emergency. Hurry. Now we only have thirteen minutes."

Which got Agatha moving, because she really did want to know if what was going on next door had anything to do with Russell Dixon's murder.

Within five minutes, they were out the front door and creeping toward the neighbor's. Gina insisted Agatha carry a mop and bucket. She was carrying a shotgun.

"What do you plan to do with that?" Agatha felt comfortable with hunting rifles since she'd grown up around them, but she didn't like the idea of Gina carrying one while they snuck onto her neighbor's property.

"I plan to not use it, but if things turn sour..."

"If what things turn sour?" Tony stepped out of the bushes, taking yet another year off Agatha's life. She'd soon be aging backwards if the night held many more surprises.

"What are you doing here?" Gina hissed.

"The same question I was going to ask you." Tony shone his flashlight on the two of them. He'd wrapped red plastic wrap around the end, and it produced a ghastly glow. "And why is Agatha wearing *Englisch* clothes?"

"I can answer for myself." Agatha straightened her t-shirt as if that would explain things. "We're undercover."

"Don't tell me you two are planning to break into McNair's."

"We don't have to break in. I know someone on the inside. What was your plan?"

"I was watching—legally, from outside the perimeter."

"Oh. There's Nate."

Before Agatha or Tony could pull her back, Gina dashed across the driveway and to the guard hut.

"She's fast for a woman her age," Agatha muttered, then darted after her.

If Nate was surprised to see all three of them, he didn't say anything. He did remind them to be back at the gate between the quarter and half hour. "The rest of the time I'm making my rounds."

"Is the house locked?"

"No. It doesn't need to be. Mr. McNair has the gate...and me."

"Have you seen anything suspicious?" Tony asked.

"Nah. Rich people are a little crazy, though. There's folks in and out all the time here."

"Anyone in particular?"

"Some investors from Houston were here last

week. Since then...no one."

Nate told them to watch their backs, hopped into his golf cart, and took off into the darkness.

"You know this is breaking and entering," Tony said as they hurried toward the house.

"Gina said it was perfectly legal if someone on the premises let us in."

"And why is Gina carrying a shotgun?"

"Says she brought it just in case, but she didn't say just in case what."

"Tell me you're not armed," he muttered.

"Of course not. I'm a pacifist." Agatha stared at the items in her hands. "Unless you count this mop and bucket. You?"

"I have a license to carry." Tony patted a bulge on his hip.

"As do I." Gina was still adamantly defending her constitutional rights.

"That license does not permit you to carry a shotgun onto someone else's property."

Agatha hushed both of them. They'd reached the front door. Tony turned them both away from what must have been a security camera. It was only then that Agatha noticed he was wearing a ball cap too, only his was black and had no permanent marker writing on the front of it.

"Pull your caps down low, and don't look up."

They stepped into a house that looked like something out of a fancy *Englisch* magazine. In front of them was an extremely large room, with a ceiling that stretched two stories high. The far wall, the one that looked out toward the river, was solid glass. To their right was a giant fireplace, and on both sides of that several animal heads including a giant deer, a mountain lion, and a zebra.

Agatha stepped closer to Tony. "Is it legal to shoot zebras?"

"Not here. He had to go overseas to get that one—at least I hope he did." Tony moved past them into the room, then turned and faced Gina and Agatha, crossing his arms and planting his feet shoulder width apart, as if daring them to shove their way past him. Plainly, they wouldn't have to do that. The room was huge. They could dodge to the left and right.

"Before we take another step, before you incriminate all of us, tell me your plan."

Agatha pulled in a deep breath to explain, but Gina beat her to it.

"We know the Amish guests were invested in Dixon's company." She put air quotes around the last two words.

"But we don't think they knew what they were getting into," Agatha quickly added.

"I'm checking into that. I told you—"

"Everyone leaves tomorrow, Tony." Gina shifted her shotgun to her left hand. "We need to solve this tonight."

"You can't solve a mystery in one night because someone has travel plans."

"The boot print in the garden was facing toward my property," Agatha pointed out. She normally chose the path of caution, and she appreciated his concern, but she was ready for this to be over. If looking around McNair's house solved the mystery, she was willing to do that. It wasn't as if they were there to steal anything. "The person who made that boot print was coming from this property."

"You don't know that."

"I do. We went back and looked and it's clear someone is crossing over the fence in that area. And then there's Brooklyn's photograph, which clearly shows someone creeping onto my property—the same person who made the boot print."

"Hang on. What photograph?"

"I left a note on your door. It explained everything."

"I stopped by the house before I came here. There wasn't any note."

"We can figure out why we're doing this later," Gina muttered.

Agatha stared down at her blue jean-clad legs, then back up at Tony. "I'm sorry, but Gina's right. My guests leave tomorrow. It's better if we solve this tonight."

"Anything we find here will be inadmissible in court."

"But we'll know if we're looking the right direction. We'll learn if any of the guests are involved or if it has nothing to do with them at all. Perhaps they simply scheduled a Hill Country vacation at the wrong time."

Agatha looked around in wonder, but her mind was flipping over all that had happened in the last week. She couldn't see it yet, but she had the feeling the pieces of this puzzle were coming together.

Gina turned in a circle to take in all of the room, then faced Tony. "Whoever is doing this is trying to put Agatha out of business. I'm not going to let that happen."

"The timing is what brought it all together." Agatha attempted to swipe at her hair, then remembered she was holding a bucket.

Gina shifted her shotgun into her opposite hand. "Brooklyn was out walking by the river Wednesday morning, before dawn. She was taking pictures of the B&B, but she inadvertently caught our creeper coming onto the property."

"At the same time Dixon was arguing with the Cox brothers."

"The pictures are time stamped."

"Someone lured Dixon out of his room..." Agatha peered at Tony. "It was all in the note I left on your side door—the one you always enter your house through. I even used yellow tape so you'd be sure to see."

"Again—there was no note."

"Then someone took it, and that same person is sabotaging Agatha's business." Gina's grip on the shotgun tightened. "There's a good chance he or she killed Russell Dixon. So why don't we stop talking and start looking."

It again occurred to Agatha that she was the only one without a weapon. But then, what would she do with one? She could never hurt another person. She'd joined the church when she was a young woman and part of their *Ordnung* included a commitment to pacifism. She could never knowingly harm someone, regardless of the reason for doing so.

"Put your phone on silent," Tony said to Gina. "One of us stays with Agatha at all times since she doesn't have any way to call for help."

"I have my voice." She wanted to add that she wasn't a child and didn't need looking after, but now didn't seem the time.

"I'll go through the rooms upstairs." Gina was already headed toward the sleek curved staircase.

"We'll take the downstairs," Tony said. "Come on, Agatha. It's me and you, kid."

Agatha still felt like she'd been caught up in an *Englisch* movie, but she didn't argue. Instead, she crept along behind Tony as they slowly moved from room to room.

Chapter Thirty-one

TONY HAD no doubt that he'd soon regret what they were doing, but he also couldn't really fault their logic. Though there were many reasons for taking another life—more than he'd first thought as a young detective—most involved either passion or money. Passion was usually a quick strike and confined to the person who felt betrayed and the betrayer. Rarely were more people involved.

This felt bigger—the paint on Agatha's barn, the person who tried to run him off the road—it all pointed to an ongoing response to something. He was willing to bet that something had a dollar sign on it.

His gut told him McNair was involved. If they could find the evidence...any evidence...perhaps he'd have the knowledge to work backwards. Or he could call in an anonymous tip to the police. Since he was no longer on the force, he was just an average citizen breaking into a neighbor's home.

The thought wasn't terribly comforting.

He glanced back at Agatha, surprised at how she looked the same and at the same time totally different. She was wearing jeans and a t-shirt similar to what Gina had been wearing. She'd replaced her traditional *kapp* with a ball cap, and her hair hung in a long braid down her back.

She somehow looked younger in the *Englisch* clothes—younger, and completely out of her element.

Together they did a cursory look in the kitchen, dining area, living room, and media room. They were at the end of the hall and about to give up on the bottom floor when Agatha jiggled a doorknob and said, "It's locked."

"Let me see." He tried the doorknob, but she was right. It was locked.

"Who locks a door in their own house, when they're not there and they have a guard outside?"

"Does seem like overkill." Tony felt along the carpet, looked under a small occasional table in the hall, then ran his hand along the top of the doorframe. "Bingo."

Agatha's eyes widened in surprise and a smile spread across her face.

He placed the key into the lock, and they stepped into the room.

"Leave it open," he said. "We want to hear if anyone comes down the hall."

There was no ambient light in the room, but Tony's night vision had always been good.

"Stay here," he whispered, and then walked over to a sitting area and turned on one of the lamps. Its light bathed the room in a soft glow.

And what a room it was.

Leather furniture, dark paneling, and a well-stocked liquor cabinet set the tone. Glass encompassed the wall which looked out over the river, floor to ceiling, just like the main room. A bookcase covered the length of the opposite wall. But it was the wall facing the door that drew his attention. McNair had mounted antique rifles, swords, and crossbows from one end of the room to the other. It wasn't exactly an armory, as most of the pieces appeared to be quite old, but it was unusual.

Tony had stepped closer to admire a flintlock pistol, when Agatha called out.

"I think we found it."

"Found what?"

"Found the answer to what's going on." She stood at the far side of the room, to the right of a huge mahogany desk. Tony hurried over to her side, noting that the large table held some kind of architectural model.

254

He stood there, staring at it, unable to understand exactly what he was seeing.

"Where's my house?" Agatha whispered.

And then it all came together, the Guadalupe River along one edge of the platform, and along the other side to the south sat McNair's place, only it wasn't only McNair's house he was looking at. Next to it was a much larger structure. He leaned closer, and focused the beam of his flashlight on the model's fine print in the bottom corner.

The Guadalupe Resort,
a McNair-Bench-Hawthorne property. Headquarters.

He splayed his flashlight across the board, revealing a twenty-story hotel, cottages, cabanas, nightclub, seven swimming pools, and an amphitheater. "This covers your property, my property, and the Simpson Ranch."

"So he thought he could drive me out of business—somehow that has to be tied into Dixon's death. But what about your property? How did he plan to get that?"

Tony shook his head. "I don't know. Or maybe I do. McNair knew about Camilla's death. He even came by to offer his condolences. A few months later I received a card, telling me if I ever decided to sell— if the memories became too much—to call him and he'd give me a fair price."

"Have you considered selling?"

"I hadn't thought about it seriously. Maybe? Honestly, I couldn't see around my grief far enough to know what I wanted to do. But I might have... if your place was gone and he'd purchased the Simpson Ranch on the other side of me. I wouldn't want to be in the middle of a development like this."

"And the Simpson Ranch on the far side of you is for sale."

"They're asking too much for it. But this? This is deep pockets. They could probably swing it."

"If he started the construction all around you — if you were stuck in the middle..."

"I wouldn't put up much of a fight."

Agatha leaned toward the board, then pulled Tony's hand so that the light shone on the far left corner. "Look at this."

Tony let out a long, low whistle.

"What is that?"

"My guess? The projected construction price."

"Seventy-eight million dollars?" Agatha shook her head in disbelief, causing the long braid down her back to swing back and forth. "Would someone really invest that much?"

"I guess so. Look at this." On the other corner of the board was an Amount Raised scale. The marker was set at 39 million.

"Half. He already has half."

The immense weight that had been pressing on Tony since he'd first viewed Russell Dixon's body lifted. He'd found motive. He'd found the perpetrator. One way or another, McNair was behind all of it. "Once he has our properties, the other half of his funding would be fairly easy to acquire."

"So how does all this tie in with Russell Dixon?"

"I don't know, but I do know one thing...we just found motive. Let's get out of here."

The second they turned back toward the door, Tony knew that wasn't going to happen. Daryl McNair stood there, and he held a nine-millimeter handgun pointed directly at them. Crime was supposed to take its toll on a man, but McNair seemed to be thriving from the dark side of his life. He wore jeans and a designer fishing shirt which hung easily on his muscular frame. His expression was relaxed, almost as if he was enjoying the moment.

Tony fought the urge to go for the handgun in the paddle holster on his hip. McNair smiled, practically daring him to try it. He didn't have time. He knew that. Maybe if Agatha could distract the man.

"I see you two found my project. Isn't the model wonderful?" He flicked his gun to the left, moving them toward the windows. Nowhere to run. The windows were no use because Tony could see from where he stood that the panes were too thick to bust through.

"They're even sound proof," McNair said, as if reading his mind. "Wouldn't want all that noise from the resort filtering in."

"Did you actually kill Russell Dixon...for this?" Agatha looked more puzzled than frightened.

Tony stepped closer to her. He didn't realize until he glanced at her that they both had their hands raised. It was an instinctive posture when someone threatened you with a gun.

See? I'm no danger. My hands are empty.

Two large men dressed in black stepped into the room behind McNair. "The rest of the building is clear."

"And Luscombe?"

"I gave him the rest of the night off."

"Tomorrow I want you to fire him. If he can't keep these two out, he's not worth having around."

Tony willed Agatha to not look at him, to not give anything away. If McNair and his men hadn't found Gina, there was still hope.

"Secure them." McNair looked bored. Was the man so arrogant he considered them a mere distraction?

"It's not too late, McNair. Up until now, this is a misunderstanding, but once you kidnap us..."

"Kidnap you? Please, I have no interest in holding a burned-out cop and a religious lady captive. I'm simply going to take you to a more remote location, find out what you know, and then kill you."

Chapter Thirty-two

AGATHA FIGURED she must be in shock. She was more fascinated than terrified when one of the big, burly guys pulled out a roll of duct tape, motioned for Tony to put his arms behind his back, and proceeded to wrap the tape around and around his wrists. He removed Tony's pistol and set it on McNair's desk, then frisked him to make sure he didn't have any other weapons.

She should be frightened.

Her brain knew that.

But honestly...what good would screaming for help do at this point?

There was no one to hear, except perhaps Gina.

She glanced at Tony at the same moment the burly man moved toward her.

"Hands behind your back."

"Let her leave them in front." Tony was still holding her gaze, trying to tell her something. "She's an old woman with a bad shoulder."

She played along. "I can barely lift it some days." It wasn't a lie. She'd had shoulder impingement for years, but how did Tony know that?

"I know you're not afraid of her..."

"Who would be afraid of an *old woman*?" She emphasized the words as Tony had. She'd give him what-for about that description once they were free, and in that moment she realized the reason she wasn't afraid. She did believe they'd find a way out of this.

What that escape would be, she couldn't imagine.

"What difference does it make?" Tony added. "It's not like we can get away."

Burly guy looked to McNair, who shrugged. "I don't care. They get a bullet either way."

"Put your elbows together, Agatha. It's less strain on the shoulder that way." Tony used a low voice as if he were only talking to her, but she had the distinct impression he wanted McNair to hear.

"Did you do it? Did you kill Russell Dixon?" Agatha's voice was less firm than she had hoped. She cleared her throat and tried again. "What could be worth taking another life?"

"Dixon should have thanked me. He had a

miserable life, and he got in the way — just like you two are in the way."

"So all this is for your resort? For a development plan?" Tony's voice was even and calm.

Agatha had the strange thought that he'd been through a similar situation before. Or perhaps his training included how to appear unruffled. Whatever it was, she was grateful. His lack of fear helped to keep hers at bay.

"You have no idea," McNair said. "This development will make me rich — very rich. You two can't imagine what that means, I know, but it's a far better life."

"Better? What difference does it make if you have five million or twenty?"

"Proof of your ignorance, Vargas."

"And the people who live here have no say in what happens to the area?"

"If I didn't do it somebody else would. Why should someone else be the one to benefit when I've held this miserable piece of property for twenty years? Fishing and wildlife and natural resources... I've heard it all, but what it always comes down to is, how will it benefit the person talking? I'm not the only hypocrite. I'm simply an honest one."

Agatha had no idea how to answer that, and as it turned out she didn't have to. Once her hands were secured in front, McNair addressed the other burly guy.

"Put them in the back of the van. You know where to take them."

They were prodded out of the office, back through the great room, and out the front door. A white panel van idled under the portico. Agatha had the bizarre thought that perhaps someone had called an Uber, and it was waiting for them.

Burly guy pushed them into the vehicle, smirked at them, then slammed the doors shut.

Agatha found herself enshrouded in pitch-black darkness.

Well, she'd grown up on an Amish farm. Darkness was something she was accustomed to. Something she'd often found peace and comfort in—knowing that God was the maker of darkness and light, that God was beside her regardless the position of the sun, that God was her provider and helper.

Someone put the van into drive, and it shot away from McNair's house.

Tony slid over next to her.

"Are you okay?"

"*Ya*, for sure and certain...other than being bound, kidnapped, and on my way to being shot." Her voice pitched higher than usual. She fought to bring it down. "What's your plan?"

"Can you stand up?"

"Maybe."

The van was bouncing around, but once they

hit the main road, the ride smoothed out.

"Try now. Put your back against the wall, and try to push up."

The first time she made it a foot or so and landed on her bottom, but that was probably because the driver made a too-fast turn. Who had taught that young man to drive? The second attempt, she managed to get her feet underneath her. Tony was already standing beside her. "Just lean on me, and push your way up."

"Whew. Okay. What now?"

"Now I'm going to tell you how to get out of that duct tape." His voice came to her in the darkness—calm, quiet, in control. He might be worried, but he was not panicked. That did more to slow her pounding pulse than anything else could have.

"This stuff is pretty strong," she said. "I remember my *onkel* duct taping a gate shut once to keep the cows in. It actually worked."

"It is strong, which is why bad guys use it. I want you to raise your arms above your head."

She sensed he was showing her how, though in the darkness she couldn't see him. Still, friendship forged in terrible times required trust. She definitely trusted Tony Vargas.

"Okay. My arms are above my head."

"Listen to me before you try this. You're going to bring your arms down, quickly and with as much force as you can. As you do, let your arms come out at an angle, so that they brush your hips."

"Okay."

"Not straight down. That won't work. Down, with force, and at an angle."

Someone could have knocked her over with a feather when the tape gave way on the second try. "Glad the cows didn't figure this out. Now it's your turn."

"I can't do that with my arms behind me. Help me find something I can saw it up against—any kind of angle or sharp edge."

Agatha drew in her breath sharply. "Turn around. I have scissors in my pocket." When she'd changed from her dress and apron into the *Englisch* clothes, she'd emptied her pockets and put the small sewing scissors into her blue jeans pocket.

Her *schweschder* had given her the craft scissors, which came with an embroidered sheath— something she claimed would come in handy for her new venture in Texas. "Because inn owners probably always need them on hand."

Thinking of her family caused a sob to catch in her throat. She loved Texas, but she wanted to see her siblings and her children and her grandchildren again.

With a start, she realized her emotions were all over the place. She needed to pull them under control if she was going to be any help at all. Certainly Tony didn't deserve to die this way—he'd simply been helping out a neighbor.

She opened the tiny scissors, felt for the gap between his hands and went to work on his bound wrists.

When he was free, instead of rubbing his wrists, Tony put his hands on both of her shoulders. She could easily imagine his look of concern.

"Are you all right?"

"Yes. What do you think happened to Gina?"

"They didn't find her, so hopefully she's alerted the authorities."

"What do we do until they come for us?"

"We don't wait for that. We get out of here. Keep a hand on my shoulder."

He led her a few feet until they'd reached the back of the van. "Back up into the corner. I'm going to open the door, and we're going to jump."

"Yikes."

"You'll go first. Try to land in a crouch, not straight-legged. Chin to your chest and roll as soon as you hit the ground."

"Got it. Chin to chest. Won't they notice?"

It was then she became aware of the rowdy music coming from the cab of the truck, along with a rather foul odor.

"By now, they should be high from whatever they're smoking, and they won't hear us over the music. Wait for me to say go."

He must have found the latch. She heard a click and then the door opened. The interior of the van was filled with the rush of air. Those thoughts barely registered when he shouted, "Go. Now!"

His hand on her back, he gave her a good shove, and then she was tucking and rolling and hitting the ground as pain coursed through her shoulder. She sat up and fought to catch her breath when she heard Tony running toward her.

"What took you so long?"

"I waited until you were clear. I didn't want to jump on top of you."

"I appreciate that."

"Anything broken?"

"*Nein*. I don't think so, but there's going to be a bruise."

"I'll take a bruise to a bullet any day."

He helped her stand, and they both turned to face the van, whose taillights were fading from sight.

❋

Chapter Thirty-three

TONY WASN'T sure when it had happened. Maybe when they'd jumped from the van. Possibly when Daryl McNair had first pointed a gun at them. Or perhaps much earlier...perhaps it was when Agatha first ran up his back porch steps breathlessly telling him there was a dead body in Cabin 3.

Somewhere along the way, Tony had decided that he wanted to live.

His life would never be the same without Camilla.

His retirement years certainly wouldn't be what he'd always dreamed they would be.

But he was still grateful for every new day, thankful that he could draw a breath, and happy about the unexpected friend walking by his side.

Tony Vargas knew, for the first time in a long time, that he was glad to be alive.

"Will they turn back? When they discover we're gone?"

"They might."

"But we'd hear them coming."

"We would."

"Do you know where we are?"

Tony stopped in the middle of the road, put his hands on her shoulders, and turned her to the right where moonlight was sparking off water.

"The Guadalupe," she whispered. "We could walk along the banks and end up at home."

"The road is probably safer. Wouldn't want you to escape McNair's goons just to be bitten by a cottonmouth."

They proceeded to walk down the center of the deserted road.

"I still don't understand what Dixon had to do with McNair's plans for a resort."

"Neither do I, but the police will sort all that out when they arrest him."

"Unless he runs."

"Daryl McNair strikes me as too arrogant to run. He'll believe he can maneuver his way out right up to the minute they close the prison door on him when he's serving ninety-nine to life."

"And that's what he'll get?"

"No doubt about it since—"

The whine of a motorcycle split the night. Agatha jerked to the right, but Tony pulled her back. "McNair drives a Maserati."

The single light of the motorcycle lit them up, the driver skidded to a stop, and Gina Phillips jumped off. She jerked the helmet off her head and ran toward them. "You're okay. Oh, my stars." She bent over, hands on knees. "I thought...I was sure..."

Agatha pulled her friend into a hug. "We're fine. How did you find us?"

"I was coming down the stairs when I heard McNair and his hoodlums come in. I went back up, and then it was simply a matter of waiting for them to go into a different room so I could sneak back downstairs."

She'd left the bike's headlight on. Tony moved to the right and smiled when he saw her shotgun bungee-corded across the back.

"I didn't think I could outgun them three to one, so I ran to try and find Nate."

"He was still there?"

"Yeah. He knew something was up when he was suddenly given the night off, and he wasn't comfortable leaving until he'd seen or heard from us."

"But how did you follow us?" Tony asked.

"Nate had the motorcycle, which I know how to ride. He also has a drone he's been messing around with during the middle of the night when there's nothing else to do on his shift."

She tapped the Bluetooth device she was wearing. "Agatha and Tony are with me. They're okay. Yes, about three miles after the turn."

"He searched for us with the drone?" Agatha and Tony peered up at the sky, but if Nate's drone was there, they couldn't see it.

"He used the drone to follow the van. We saw them put you in it. I'm surprised I didn't run over you—I was trying to stay back, but I also was afraid of losing you. Nate's been giving me directions, but his drone..." She put a finger to the ear piece. "Police are almost here."

"What about the drone?"

"It only has a range of four miles. He was able to tell me where to turn, and then he had to pull it back. We don't know where the van went, only that it continued down this road."

The quiet of the night was split by the sound of police cruisers.

And then they were surrounded by Hunt County police officers. Tony was even glad to see Tami Griffin and Jimmy Bannister. Behind them was an ambulance.

He filled Bannister in on what he knew. Bannister radioed it to someone else, who responded that they had the van in their sights and were directing other officers toward it.

So they'd called in a helicopter.

That was surprising.

Tony wouldn't have considered him and Agatha to be that big a priority, but then Bannister met his gaze and nodded once.

Tony felt a new respect for the man. He might be arrogant and over-eager but he did his job thoroughly, and because of that Daryl McNair would be in a jail cell before morning light.

He wasn't absolutely certain about every detail of what would happen next—though with his years on the force he had a pretty good idea.

What he knew for sure was that the nightmare was over.

❋

Chapter Thirty-four

AGATHA AND Tony stepped out of the police cruiser. Officer Griffin blipped the siren once, then drove away.

"Long day," Tony said, his hand at her elbow as they walked up the steps to her porch.

"But a productive one."

"I suppose you could see it that way. How's the shoulder?"

"Fine. How's your hip?"

"I'll survive."

She turned to him to try and voice the many feelings tumbling through her heart and mind. Now might not be the best time, but she'd learned not to wait. Nothing was certain in this life, only in the next one—their heavenly one. Best to tell him now that she appreciated his help, that she was relieved to have a friend like him next door. She'd interrupted his quiet and peaceful life, and turned it into something much more chaotic. She didn't know how she'd make it up to him, but she planned to try if it meant baking him pies every week until he begged her to stop.

She was wondering where to start, when the sound of her back porch door slapping shut startled them both.

They jogged around the corner of the house in time to see two people sprinting down the path that led to the river. Tony took off at a run, Agatha lagging a bit behind. She stopped at the path where it turned away from Cabin 3, where all this had started. She stopped and put her hand to her side and pulled in a deep breath.

Tony would be fine.

He had help.

The Cox brothers had stepped out of the river in time to stop Jasmine and Xavier. She'd thought Mason and Paxton were gone—their note said as much, but there they were. With the Cox brothers on one side and Tony on the other, the two dropped the bags they were carrying and held up their hands.

Fifteen minutes later, they were in Agatha's kitchen.

Tony put in a call to the police department and told them there was no hurry...to finish up with McNair first. He'd make sure the Coopers didn't get away.

Mason and Paxton had trooped into the house as well, dripping water all over Agatha's floor. Tony gave them a pointed look, and they stepped outside and removed their waders. But honestly, Agatha didn't care about water on her floor. She could clean that up the next day, though perhaps now would be better. No need in surviving a kidnapping just to fall and break a leg in her own kitchen. After she wiped up the water, she sat down at the table.

"I don't understand. You seem like such a nice couple."

"Nice doesn't cut it, Agatha. Not everyone has a place on the river." Jasmine's bitterness seeped from her like water through a sieve.

"We were robbed, if you want to know the truth. Robbed by McNair." Xavier slouched down in his chair.

Agatha resisted the urge to remind him to sit up straight. No doubt a sore back would be the least of his problems.

"McNair was looking for investors." Xavier looked from Tony to Agatha then back to Tony. "He made it sound so lucrative, so certain. When he offered to let us in, how could we turn it down?"

Agatha probably should have kept quiet, but at this point, she was so tired her thoughts bubbled out of her head without consent. "But why? Why would you risk everything for money?"

"Says the person who has plenty of it." Jasmine

shook her head. "You have no idea what it's like. You've always had family, always had plenty to eat. Xavier and I...we fought our way out of the south side of Houston."

"Which doesn't justify falling in with a killer," Tony said.

"We didn't know he was a killer!" Xavier crossed his arms and glared at them. "This wasn't supposed to happen. Dixon was sent here to scare you away—"

"Was that why he was snooping around in my pantry?"

"I guess. Maybe he was going to mess with your breaker box or something. One way or another, he was supposed to convince you to sell your place, and if that wasn't possible to sabotage it. His job was to ensure that the city came out and closed you down."

"There's no reason for them to shut me down."

"There would have been, if Dixon hadn't gotten cold feet."

Tony sat back, arms crossed. He didn't think these two would be running again. They both looked exhausted. "You came here because Dixon was here."

"We were supposed to back him up—make sure he did what he was hired to do." Jasmine threw a hate-filled look toward Mason and Paxton, who were blocking both exits from the kitchen. "This would've worked if he'd stuck to the plan. Instead he told us this place reminded him of his grandpa's. Said he couldn't lie anymore, not after what he did with your brother's case."

"I know about the resort, but I still don't understand what that has to do with my *bruder*'s death. Did McNair...did McNair hire that woman to run into him?"

Jasmine snorted.

"Nah. That was just good timing." As if suddenly hearing her words, she looked temporarily chastened. "Sorry, I didn't mean it that way."

"I think you did," Tony said, his voice hard and his expression cold.

"It was good timing is all. McNair made your brother an offer for this place, but Samuel said he wasn't interested in money. He was interested in creating a *haven of rest*. Those were his exact words. Can you believe it?"

Agatha met Tony's gaze. "*Ya*. I can."

"All McNair had to do was have Dixon assigned to the case, ensure the wrongful death claim was denied, and this place would default to the bank."

"McNair would swoop in and buy it cheap."

"Except I came along." Agatha's thoughts scrambled to put all the pieces together.

The Cox brothers had been largely silent, but now Paxton stepped forward, rubbing his brow as if to ward off a headache.

276

"I thought you two were gone," Agatha said.

Mason smiled at his brother. "We were, or we pretended to be. Then we hid down at the river to help you catch whoever did this."

"It seemed to us that we were mixed up in the middle, but we couldn't explain how." Paxton stuffed his hands in his pockets. "We didn't even understand what happened. Dixon came to our cabin—accused us of shadowing him, of being the backup in case he didn't finish the job. We didn't know what he was talking about. The guy started shouting. He was super agitated. We finally told him to leave."

"The argument Jasmine and Xavier heard..."

"Yeah, we didn't have to make that part up." Jasmine massaged her forehead with her fingertips. "We didn't know McNair was going to kill Dixon."

"Why didn't you just talk to me?" Tony's voice was puzzled, his question directed to Mason and Paxton. "Might have saved us all a lot of trouble."

Mason was shaking his head before Tony finished speaking. "Having an argument with a guy before he turns up dead doesn't look too good on a witness report."

"He didn't know we were the ones here to watch him," Xavier admitted.

"McNair used you to kill him." Tony spoke slowly, his eyes tracking from Xavier to Jasmine and back again. "When Dixon had a change of heart..."

"He threatened to report everything to the police," Jasmine said.

"So McNair resorted to Plan B. You two were Plan B. He had you exchange the breakfast food. And maybe he had you break in during the argument and steal Dixon's EpiPen, computer and cell phone."

Xavier and Jasmine exchanged worried looks.

"We're not saying anything else," Jasmine said.

"And we want a lawyer." Xavier covered his face with his hands, and neither of them said another word.

Tami Griffin showed up ten minutes later. "Texas Rangers have custody of McNair. He's already lawyered up, which won't matter. There's enough evidence in his cabin alone to convict him of murdering Russell Dixon. We won't need his confession, but if he's smart enough to admit it, he might get life instead of the death penalty."

"What happened to the two burly guys?"

"Tommy and Trent Riggs?" Tami's eyebrows shot up and a smile spread across her face. "State troopers caught them. At the moment they're being held for DUI, but they'll transfer to us tomorrow for additional charges."

For the second time that day, Agatha and Tony stood on the front porch watching a Hunt Police Officer drive away.

Agatha had forgotten about the Cox brothers until she turned and saw them still standing on the porch. "What are you two doing still here?"

"Here?" Paxton asked.

Mason pulled back in surprise. "We helped you catch those guys."

"Yeah, we're on your side in this. We told you—we were in the river, watching and ready to catch whoever did this."

Tony looked toward the heavens, as if he might find more patience there. "What Agatha means is, what are you doing at her Bed-and-Breakfast? It's obvious you're not fishing, though you seem to be in your waders pretty often."

The brothers shared a look.

"Might as well tell them," Mason said.

"Not like we found anything anyway."

"Personally, I'm ready to get back home."

"Yep, panning's a lot harder than our real jobs."

"Panning?" Tony shook his head in disbelief. "You were panning the Guadalupe?"

"We came across this website pretty much by accident—Hidden Treasures. If you were willing to pay, the website gave you clues to lost riches."

"Lost riches?" Agatha had thought this evening couldn't get any stranger, but it just did.

"You know—sunken treasure, buried money, even streams that hadn't been panned out. The website said there was gold here."

"Practically guaranteed it."

"Maybe not here exactly, but along this stretch."

Tony held up his hand to stop them. "There's no gold here, guys. Though there are a lot of fish."

"So we found out." Mason momentarily looked dejected, but then he seemed to catch his second wind. "Still, you have a good place, Agatha. Best vacation I've ever spent with this goober."

Paxton sidestepped his brother's light punch. "Maybe next time we'll come back and fish."

"And sleep...man, I could use some sleep."

The brothers walked off around the porch and to their cabin.

"Another mystery solved," Agatha said.

"You need to get some rest."

"Seriously?" Agatha motioned to the east. "I have guests to feed. Everyone who wasn't involved with McNair will be wondering where breakfast is, and in case you have forgotten, I do run a Bed-and-Breakfast—"

"A haven of rest."

"Indeed." Agatha felt a lump in her throat, maybe for the first time that night. Her brother had died because of a random accident, but she would find a way to see that his dream came true. She wasn't going to run back to Indiana just because a crazy neighbor killed one of her guests and tried to kill her. "I should go start cooking."

"Then I insist on helping."

"Seriously? Do you even know how to cook?"

"I can make a mean cup of coffee."

Chapter Thirty-five

Six days later, Tony and Agatha sat across from Kiara at the corner table in Sammi's. Same table, but the day felt very different to Tony—full of hope and possibility.

He stabbed his apple pie as if it had offended him. "I can't believe you're representing the Coopers."

"Which reminds me, did they take the note I left for Tony? The note telling him Gina and I were going over to McNair's?"

"They did. Apparently McNair told them to watch you closely and intervene when necessary."

Agatha squirreled her nose, as if she'd smelled something distasteful.

"They need a good lawyer," Kiara said,

pointing a finger at Tony. "And I have it on record that you once said I'm a good one."

"I'm glad you are." Agatha shrugged when Tony shot her a look of surprise. "I'd like to see Jasmine and Xavier get a second chance."

"Mostly they're guilty of being stupid and gullible. Even when they replaced your breakfast with the one that McNair gave them, they thought it was going to give him food poisoning and take him out of the picture. They didn't know they were killing him."

"Or so they told you." Tony finished the pie and pushed away the plate.

"Yours is better," he assured Agatha, who rolled her eyes and motioned for Kiara to continue.

"Also, they were smart enough to keep a backup of all the emails McNair sent them."

"Why would he risk laying out his plan in an email?"

"As you've pointed out more than once, he's arrogant. He couldn't imagine anyone turning on him."

"And if they did, he'd just kill them."

"Exactly." Kiara sipped her coffee and ate a tiny piece of her peach cobbler. "McNair is a street thug from way back. He's actually changed his name more than once and reinvented himself. It was McNair who got Dixon started on his Ponzi scheme. McNair had run something similar in New Jersey and Georgia. Both times he slipped through the net authorities set for him, moved, and changed his name."

"People like that never learn. They move and do the same thing all over again." Tony had seen a lot of crime in his years on the force. Ponzi schemes were among the worst. They took away a person's pride as well as their future resources.

"Along the way he had more and more money from previous victims, and his scams grew in scale and audacity."

Agatha cocked her head to the side. "Did he really have investors committed for half the money of the resort?"

"He did, and from what I can tell those investors are on the up and up. McNair isn't the first person to want to put up a resort in the Texas Hill Country."

"The Hill Country is special because it's remote, with fewer people and less traffic. We don't want a resort." Tony crossed his arms in defiance.

"Tell that to the people in Fredericksburg. The one there is set to open next year." Kiara accepted a refill on her coffee from the waitress, added cream but no sugar, and tapped the spoon against the mug. Smiling at Agatha, she said, "Better watch out. You're getting more competition for your Bed-and-Breakfast every day."

Agatha waved that thought away. "Amish folk like this area. It's a *gut* place to relax. A *gut* place to reconnect with nature, and they can do that at my Bed-and-Breakfast. A resort isn't exactly a plain and simple vacation."

"Her customer base is solid," Tony agreed. "That's why she's adding on to the B&B."

"Really?"

"Just a few more cabins. My family in Indiana sent me more money they wanted to invest. That, combined with what I've earned so far, gives me the funds to do some things I thought I wouldn't be able to for a few years."

"You can finish the shuffle board courts," Tony said.

"And add some outdoor grills, a playground for the *youngies*—tubes and kayaks, too."

Kiara cocked her head, smiled at them both, and nodded her approval. "Sounds like you have a busy season ahead of you."

"It's all *gut*. Plus I have a new fishing guide for my guests." Agatha bumped shoulders with Tony.

"And I can walk to work." Tony laughed. It felt good to be involved in life again, and late summer was a perfect time to be a fishing guide. Better yet, fall was around the corner—temperatures would be pleasant, colors would be changing, and he had no doubt the fish would be biting. "It's a win-win for everyone."

"Well, I'm happy for you both." Kiara drained her coffee and stood. Dropping money on the table, she said, "I've got this. After all, you sent me two new clients."

"All right, but come by for dinner some time. You said you would."

"And I keep my promises." Kiara shook hands with Tony then turned toward Agatha. "You have my number if you need me."

"Let's hope that doesn't happen. I'm out of the murder mystery business."

Tony knew she meant it. Agatha was a paradox to him. She enjoyed things simple and slow, but she'd certainly risen to the occasion when matters called for it. He thought of that moment he'd jumped out of the van, of all the things he'd meant to say to her, of how it seemed Agatha Lapp had woken him from a long sleep.

But as they walked toward his vehicle, he realized he had plenty of time to share those things, and besides—the smile from Agatha told him she already knew.

"There are some things I still don't understand," she admitted.

"Not sure I can answer your questions, but throw them at me. I did meet with Bannister yesterday, and he was more forthcoming than he has been in the past."

"That commendation from the mayor made him happy—at least he looked pleased on the front of the Hunt County News."

"The reporter did a good job, and maybe Bannister is seeing that I'm not a threat to him." Tony crossed his arms and leaned his back side against the truck. Agatha did the same. "Honestly, it's not only Bannister who changed. I've finally realized that he may not do the job the way I did it, but he's still a good cop and a good detective."

He waited and let Agatha gather her thoughts. He'd learned a lot about Agatha Lapp in the last two weeks, since she'd fled up his porch steps crying for help. She was kind and outgoing, and she didn't start talking until she had her thoughts lined up.

"I keep seeing Dixon's body and his room. I don't understand how it happened. Why did he toss his own clothes? Why did he go out the back door? Did he cry out for help?"

"I think you're asking three different things. The first is how."

"*Ya*, I suppose so."

"We know McNair had one of his goons— they're still arguing about who did it—cross the property line near your barn."

"The boot print."

"Yup. McNair had warned Dixon that he had a backup, that he'd take care of things without his help if he had to. He hinted quite strongly that two people staying at your place would take over the operation."

"Dixon thought it was the Cox brothers."

"McNair wanted him to think that. He had one of his goons sneak into Dixon's cabin while he was confronting the Cox brothers."

"That was a diversion."

"Completely. While he was out of the room, either Tommy or Trent Riggs snuck in, found the EpiPen, and took it. They also snagged his phone and computer."

"Wouldn't Dixon have noticed that his clothing was a mess?"

"I doubt it was at that point...this is all conjecture, mind you. We may never know the exact details."

"Go on."

"McNair then had Xavier switch out the breakfast after you left it on the porch."

"They were supposed to be hiking."

"Right. Instead they drove down the road, parked, and walked back."

"Then they ran back upstairs and pretended to be filling their hydration packs."

"No doubt. Once the breakfast was swapped, all they had to do was hope Dixon would take the bait."

"And McNair made this decision because Dixon backed out of the plan...the plan to sabotage my place?"

"We know that for certain. When the police arrived at the cabin—"

"The place McNair was going to kill us."

"Right. They found Dixon's laptop and phone. It's one of the ways Bannister was able to put the events together." He nudged her shoulder. "And don't go blabbing this to the paper. It stays between you and me."

"Oh, *ya*. I've turned down all interview requests." The clip-clop of a buggy horse drew their attention across the road. Agatha waved at one of her church members, but she didn't seem in any hurry to go.

"After Dixon ate the muffin, what happened then?"

Some victims needed to know the details in order to move on. He hoped what he told Agatha would help her, not cause more nightmares. "Consuming the peanut-laced muffin would have very quickly triggered Dixon's allergic reaction. He would have experienced trouble breathing, at which point he catapulted out of bed, dragging the covers with him—"

"Knocking over the coffee mug."

"He spent precious seconds searching for his EpiPen—"

"Which had already been stolen."

"...and his phone."

"But why did he go out the back door?"

"He panicked. If he'd gone out the front door, it's still doubtful anyone could have helped him."

"You're certain?" Now she raised her eyes to his, and he understood what this was about. He reached out and tucked a stray hair into her *kapp*.

"You couldn't have saved him, Agatha. Even if he'd come out on the front porch."

She nodded, and Tony thought he saw tears in her eyes—tears for a man who was trying to sabotage her business and ruin her life.

"Next he would have experienced a sudden drop in blood pressure, an increased heart rate, and unconsciousness."

"That's why he looked as if he'd been running, as if he was reaching out for help."

"Yes." There was no use sugarcoating this for her.

Agatha closed her eyes a moment. He suspected she was saying a prayer for Russell Dixon and whatever family he might have had.

When she opened her eyes, she reached up and patted him on the shoulder. "Thank you, Tony." Then she turned, walked around the truck, and climbed into the passenger seat.

"Ready to go home?" he asked.

"*Ya.* I am."

Chapter Thirty-six

IT WAS the first Monday in September when Agatha and Gina finished the pocket garden as the sun kissed the horizon. A soft light splayed across the pavers, landscape plants, birdbath, and bench.

"This is nice." Gina stood with her hands on her hips. "Your brother, he would have liked it."

"You met Samuel?"

"Only once. He'd come to town for supplies for a chicken coop. This was when I was working at the hardware store. He seemed like a real nice guy."

Agatha turned to look at the chicken coop, which was now overflowing with marigolds and monkey grass. Everything looked nice. It looked good. She would always remember Samuel and Deborah in her heart, but this was a nice way to use that memory to bless others. As they turned to go, Agatha put her hand on the bronze plate that rested waist high on a cedar pole Tony had cemented into the ground.

Samuel and Deborah's haven of rest.
May God's peace fill your soul.

She would always miss her brother, but it felt good and right that he would be remembered.

As for Agatha, she'd found her own haven of rest nestled along the Guadalupe River. As she and Gina walked back toward the main house, she saw a light go on in Tony's kitchen. Soon he'd be over, and they'd enjoy a glass of tea on the porch as they watched night settle over the hills. It was a good life, and one she planned to enjoy.

The End

❋

Author's Note

THIS BOOK is dedicated to my friend, Russell Dixon. He's been asking me to "kill him off" for years. The character in this story in no way resembles the real guy. Thanks for the laughs, Russell!

I'd like to thank Beth Scott for the use of her cat Fonzi, and others from my Friday morning prayer group who will find their names sprinkled throughout this story. You all are always on my heart and mind. A special thanks to Gina. You very much inspired my character!

As is always the case, I owe a large debt to my pre-readers: Kristy and Janet. Teresa, you did a fabulous job on the editing. Jenny, I absolutely adore the cover you created. My family deserves an award for every single book I finish. You all are the best.

I'm grateful to Center Point, who acquired the large print rights for this book before it actually existed. I appreciate your confidence in me.

And a heartfelt shout-out to all my readers who asked for another cozy mystery. It has been too long, and I hope you enjoyed this story enough to ask me to write more.

And finally ...*always giving thanks to God the Father for everything, in the name of our Lord Jesus Christ* (Ephesians 5:20).

Blessings,

Vannetta

✾

About the Author

VANNETTA CHAPMAN writes inspirational fiction full of grace. She is a PW and USA Today bestselling author of over thirty novels in a variety of genres, including Amish romances, Amish mysteries, romantic suspense, and dystopian. Vannetta is also an ACFW Carol Award winner for best mystery of the year (2012). She teaches college-level English and currently resides in the Texas Hill Country. For more information, visit her at www.VannettaChapman.com.

Share your thoughts with Vannetta at
vannettachapman@gmail.com

Read Vannetta's blog or sign up for her newsletter
at www.VannettaChapman.com

❋

Also by Vannetta Chapman

The Shipshewana Amish Mysteries
Falling to Pieces
A Perfect Square
Material Witness

The Amish Village Mysteries
Murder Simply Brewed
Murder Tightly Knit
Murder Freshly Baked

The Amish Bishop Mysteries
What the Bishop Saw
When the Bishop Needs an Alibi
Who the Bishop Knows

Find these and more at
https://vannettachapman.com/books/amish-mystery/

Made in the USA
Monee, IL
09 March 2021

MAR 1 9 2021